I0461452

# THE OUTLAW'S LETTER

## *Lockets & Lace*

## BOOK 15

## BY ANGELA RAINES

Copyright © 2019 All rights reserved by Doris A McCraw
writing as Angela Raines
All rights reserved.

# DEDICATION

This book is dedicated to
The hard-working authors of the Sweet Americana
Sweethearts blog who provide the world with sweet/clean
historical romances about North Americans between 1820
and 1929.

This book is also dedicated to the men and women who
traveled and settled the area we know as the West. To the
owners and editors of Prairie Rose Publications, Livia J
Reasoner, Cheryl Moss Pierson, who gave a fledgling
author the confidence and support to follow her dreams.
To my parents who always supported me, who told me I
could do anything I set my mind to.

## ACKNOWLEDGMENTS

This book is part of a multi-author series sponsored by the authors who write for the Sweet Americana Sweethearts blog. My appreciation and thanks go to those other authors who helped develop the Lockets & Lace series of books.

A special thank you goes to
Julia Wilcox and Dianne Hartshorn for proof-reading this manuscript,
*and to*
CarpeLibrum Book Design for the cover design.
*and*
Josephine Blake for formatting help when it was most needed.
*and*
The Thursday Night Improv Group,
this book would not be here without the help of all of you!

.

## DISCLAIMER

All the characters described in this story are fictional. They are not based on any real persons, past or present. Any resemblance to real persons, living or deceased, is coincidental and unintended.

# CHAPTER
*One*

"Well, we made it, Odysseus," Harriett 'Hetty' Osgood remarked as she rode up to the Bucket of Blood on South Union Street in Pueblo, Colorado. The sun was slipping away behind the mountains to the west, painting the sky with blues, grays, and oranges.

Tying off Odysseus, the horse she'd raised from a young colt, Hetty stepped into the shadows, adjusting the bindings on her chest and torso. As she worked to make sure they were secure, she felt her locket press against the area around her collar bone. She'd fallen in love with it the moment her grandmother gave it to her.

Grandmams had bought it in St. Joe, at The Bavarian Jewelry and Watch Repair shop, for her twelfth birthday. "Harriett," Grandmams told her after she opened the gift, "there are going to be people who say you are homely. Others who will tease you, make you try to fit in. You hold true to who you are and don't settle. It's better to be a spinster than to settle just to be married." Grandmams had given her a huge hug, adding, "You follow those words written in there, they will guide you through life." Engraved inside the locket 'I Corinthians 13:13'.

Hetty had taken Grandmams' words to heart. As a spinster, she knew she'd never have the love others claimed, so she'd made a place for herself in the world where she could do the most good. Now, she hoped she was doing the right thing. She admitted it felt right, but she also was thrilled to have taken this short adventure.

Once the bindings were back in place, she readjusted the pistol on her left hip, butt facing toward the right. By traveling cross-country, she hoped she was suitably dirty and looked like the young man she was trying to emulate. Despite what others thought, Hetty was thankful her father had taught her how to handle the gun.

"You probably ain't never gonna have a man, bein' as outspoken and plain as you are, so you need to be able to take care o' yerself," he'd said to her when he first began teaching her how to use the weapon. His words had hurt, but he and her mother had been right. When they died, she'd left to take the teaching job in Kiowa Wells. She loved her students, but she'd always wanted to live an adventure before she died.

"I need to get this letter to my brother Grant before I die," the man who'd stumbled into her school room said. "It will explain." When Hetty had started to rise, his hand shot out, grabbing her wrist. He whispered, "Tell him it's from Harrison". He had slumped back and Hetty had gone for Doc Josie and her husband Will, the town marshal.

As Doc Josie worked on his upper left shoulder where the bullet had lodged, he'd mumbled, "Bucket of Blood, meet him there."

Hetty, who had offered to help, had turned to Josie. "Wonder if he means the saloon in Pueblo?"

"And how do you know about a place like that?" Josie

had asked, a twinkle in her eye.

Turning red, Hetty hedged, "Heard the men talking outside the window one night." Both she and Josie knew there was more to the story, but they just nodded as Josie's husband Will walked in. He had gone out to try and backtrack Harrison, hoping to find who and where he had been shot. He had come back without finding anything, but told the two women he would head out again tomorrow. Harrison, had passed out after handing Hetty the letter, and other than the muttered words, had not awakened.

Now here she was, hoping that she had guessed right and Harrison's brother was here. She sighed, hoping she wouldn't have to stay or come back to the saloon after tonight. She wanted to find Grant, deliver the letter then get back to her students.

Walking back to Odysseus, Hetty rubbed his neck, whispering in his ear, "Wish me luck." She knew she was going to need it. When she thought about it, she really was looking for a needle in a bale of hay. She hoped Grant looked like his brother. Well, she was here and would give it her best. If she failed, at least she had tried.

With a swagger she almost felt, Hetty entered the saloon. She found herself a place at the end of the bar, near the door. Signaling the bartender over, Hetty watched the tall, slim man limp over. His skin so pale he looked like he'd never seen the sun.

"What's your poison?" he asked, looking Hetty over, adding, "are you old enough to..."

"Beer," Hetty interrupted, "and yes, I'm old enough. Now how about that beer?" Hetty continued, making sure her naturally low voice was even lower. Turning to observe the room, Hetty noticed it was still fairly quiet. Those that were lounging at the tables and the bar looked like regulars. With luck she could swallow enough beer to blend in, but not so much that she became ill while ferreting out the information she needed.

Her friends, Josie and Will, expressed concern about her taking on the risk of finding Grant. At the same time, she felt they understood her need to make the effort. Will argued he'd be a better choice, but Hetty stood her ground. Of course, it was because of Will she had an idea of what Grant looked like. There was an old handbill with Grant's description, and Hetty realized the brothers were very similar. Grant's crime wasn't major like murder, but had been for cattle rustling. Hetty was proud of standing her ground. Still, she felt uncomfortable standing in the saloon, but she had made her choice and despite the vile brew she was sipping, she was still standing her ground.

As the night took a tighter grip on the town, the place started filling up. The smell of stale beer, smoke and unwashed bodies increased with each man walking in. Watching the antics of the men at the bar, listening to the conversations, Hetty hoped someone might give her a clue to where outlaws might spend time. If she didn't find Grant here, she would go there. She did learn this place was where a lot of undesirables spent time.

Two hours later, Hetty was working on her second beer. The way the night was going, the thought of doing the same thing tomorrow night almost made her want to give up. She'd managed to move to the corner end of the bar. Now, away from most of the drinkers, Hetty felt a bit more comfortable. She didn't want to attract attention, just wanted to listen in the hope of hearing something.

Hetty thought about contacting marshal Desmond on her trip here, but discarded the idea. If she went to the law, all she would do is alert the very people she needed to glean information from. But after watching and experiencing tonight, Hetty was seriously considering contacting Desmond. She was preparing to leave, when a bearded man strolled in. At first Hetty thought it was just another customer, disappointed again. But something caught her eye and she jerked her head back toward the man. Something in the way he moved and his profile caught her eye.

She'd seen him before, but not the way he looked now. It had been twelve years ago, back in Kentucky. Her stomach clenched, her hand started to shake. Fear made her grasp the beer she'd put down when she was preparing to leave. Hetty looked down at her drink. Out of the corner of her eye, Hetty saw the man turn her way. The look in his eye was like a snake getting ready to strike. He started her way, effectively blocking her from escaping. *Well, if I can't get out of here, then acting scared will do me no good,* Hetty thought.

Taking a big swallow, Hetty turned and stared at the man, holding her ground by sheer will.

"Frank, where's my drink?" he shouted as he reached the small space along the bar where Hetty stood. Glancing her way, he smiled, really more like a sneer. Reaching to grab the drink the bartender placed on the bar. "Kid, you look familiar," the man commented, looking Hetty over from head to toe. "Don't know where I've seen you before, but I'll remember," he threatened as he walked toward the poker table at the back of the room.

*Now what are you going to do?* Hetty thought. She was torn between staying and leaving. If she stayed and the man kept staring at her, he would soon remember.

At the table he'd seated himself where he could see her. That she was in men's clothing and passing herself off as a young man might delay him for a while, but eventually he would remember. Her skin crawled every time he looked her way. Hetty knew there were others in the saloon that might also be wanted. She thought again of going to marshal Desmond, but what if he'd done his time and been released from prison early for good behavior? Minutes passed, her heartbeat getting louder and louder in her ears. So focused on the bearded man, Hetty almost missed seeing Grant come in. At least she believed it was Grant. He looked enough like Harrison to be a twin, although he was eighteen months older. The man was dirtier, with longer hair and stubble on his cheeks, but Hetty was sure she'd found him.

Hetty started toward Grant, when the bearded man's eyes took on a look that Hetty knew was trouble. His chair scraped back as he stood. To Hetty the sound was loud, despite all the noise echoing through the establishment. His actions told Hetty she had a few minutes before he would be on top of her, possibly destroying her disguise. She could not let that happen. Moving quickly, Hetty casually moved to the door, intentionally running into the man she hoped was Grant.

"Grant Davis?" she whispered. The look of surprise in his eyes told her what she needed to know. "I have something from your brother," her voice still a whisper, "Meet me outside." Then in a louder voice, Hetty said, "Sorry mister must have had a bit too much," as she weaved out the door. Once the night air hit her, she took a deep breath. Odysseus stood patiently. She was waiting for Grant when the door burst open and the bearded man shouted. Without hesitation, Hetty mounted, heading out of town. Odysseus was hitting his stride when a shout went up behind her, followed by a shot. Ducking automatically, Hetty leaned forward. "Keep going boy, we've gotta get out of here."

# CHAPTER
*Two*

G rant stood just inside the door, unable to move. To be accosted he understood, but called my name by a stranger who then vanished startled him.

He was roughly pushed aside as a huge man ran out the door, pulling his pistol and firing as the sound of rushing hooves echoed away.

Grant had just regained his balance when he heard the shot. "What the —?" He muttered, wondering who had gotten on the wrong side of the man Grant recognized as Boggs.

Taking over the spot vacated by Hetty, he'd just ordered when Conover 'Con' Boggs walked back in, cursing. "If it's the last thing I do I'll get that little…" At which point he pushed up to the bar. "Give me a double shot o' rye."

The barkeep rushed to fill the order, which Con

drained in one gulp. Banging the glass down, he bellowed, "Another, and $50 to any man who will help me ride down that polecat."

Grant was tempted. He was low on funds. Chasing down the folks who could clear him of the charges against him—thanks to his mother and brother—had cost more than he'd planned.

Thoughts of his brother brought back the reason he was here. He'd received word that his brother wanted to see him, to help him. Grant had hesitated, but thought he might as well see what Harrison wanted. It would also give him some satisfaction to ask Harry why. Why had he lied, why did he hate him? He'd come to the Bucket of Blood the last three days, but Harry was long overdue. Tonight was the last night, then he would resume his quest. Then he remembered the whispered words of the kid who'd run into him.

Seeing the big man next to him, Grant asked, "What happened?" He'd seen Con around these past couple of days, recognizing him for what he was. Grant was now on speaking terms with him. Grant hoped to gain his confidence and perhaps find out the whereabouts of some of the people he was looking for.

"What's it matter to you Grant?" Con snarled.

"Just curious, no other reason."

"That polecat, or someone who looked a lot like him, sent me to prison. Swore I'd make that person pay," Con finished, then downed the second drink, placing his dollar on the bar.

"For all those going hunting with me," he shouted, "let's ride."

Ten men headed out the door, running into each other as they crowded out.

"You coming?" Con asked.

"I'll catch up. Need some food."

"Well, I'll see you if I see you," Con replied, following the others out the door.

The fact that Con let his comment go without being angry or trying to convince him otherwise gave Grant a moment of unease. Grant knew his reputation as a tracker was known and figured Con knew it also. Grant had changed his looks as much as possible, but Con hadn't been fooled. Even the kid who bumped into him had guessed. The knowledge made Grant jumpy. He didn't want anything stopping him on his quest.

The whole affair dampened what appetite Grant had. Still, he knew if he didn't eat now, who knew when food would show up again. Calling the barkeep over, Grant said "I'll take whatever the special is, if you have any left."

"All we have is what's left from the free lunch," the barkeep said.

Grant nodded and headed down to the end of the bar where he saw some pickled eggs and crackers. Grabbing a couple of eggs and a few crackers, he walked back to his end of the bar and between sips of beer ate his food. It wasn't much, but more than he'd had in the last twelve hours.

*Con must've been really angry to head out and try to track someone in the dark,* Grant thought. Following that thought, Grant wondered who the young man was. When the barkeep returned to his end of the bar Grant asked, "Know who that young man was who was standing here before me?"

The barkeep shook his head, "Never seen him before, but the way he nursed his drinks I'd say he wasn't much of a drinker and pretty sure he was looking for someone."

"Thanks." The barkeep's words struck Grant. Maybe the young man had been looking for him. If that were the case, perhaps he needed to find that person. Following that thought was the fact that it was probably the young man that Con was after. The thought chilled Grant. What was it the kid had said, "I have something from you brother".

Grant called the barkeep back over, "Any idea who

Con was after?" He had a suspicion, but if someone else verified his suspicions, he would follow that hunch. Besides Con had been a regular at the Bucket of Blood lately. Grant was sure the barkeep had kept an eye on him.

"Don't know for sure, but he kept staring at the young fella standin' where you are now."

"Thanks."

His suspicions verified, Grant stuffed the rest of this food down and headed for the door. If Con caught that kid, he'd never find out how that kid had known him or why he purposely ran into him. Throwing his two bits on the bar, Grant went out the door

Mounting up, Grant tried to remember which direction the hooves sounded just before Con fired his pistol. Con probably would not be able to track the person at night. That meant that Grant could perhaps find the kid first, if he started in that general direction.

# CHAPTER
*Three*

G rant headed into the darkness, following the direction he believed the hoofbeats were heading as they'd left the saloon. Soon blackness shrouded him, silent except for the sound of Nelly's hoof falls. The moon wasn't yet up, so he was tracking by instinct. He put himself in the place a young man would be if he was riding for his life. It was a feeling he knew all too well. He didn't hurry. To hurry could prove hazardous for the young man and perhaps himself.

Grant hoped the young man had sense enough to know this wasn't a game, that the man on his tail was not playing.

Growing up, his family called themselves the 'Davis Gang'. His father had created "the game" to teach he and his brother to avoid detection. His father told them, "The west is still a wild place, and you never know when man or animal might be after you."

Grant had been very good at their game. That skill, and so many other reasons led his mother to begin to hate him even more than she had when he was younger. He never understood, although he'd tried at first to gain her love. Anything he did only seemed to make her hate him more.

As he had gotten older, he knew the outlaw life was not what he wanted. But no matter how he tried to distance himself from his mother, she had continued to make his life hell. She'd taken to calling his brother Grant instead of his real name, Harrison. Nothing she did made sense to him then, and it didn't now.

He felt thankful for that early game, it had saved him many times. He'd tried to break with the family after his father died, although he'd started trying to leave when he was about fifteen. That was almost ten years ago. He'd been lucky until his mother had helped to convict him of cattle rustling. He'd not done it, but she's set a trap he hadn't seen. Two and a half years in prison, thanks to her.

Even at an early age he began reading, working to increase his knowledge. He wanted to make something of his life. Find a good woman, settle down, have children and a steady job. Instead he was chasing after a fool of a kid when what he wanted was to clear his name. What woman would take him with the reputation and name of outlaw?

"We're fools, and we'll probably meet a fool's end." Then with a self-conscious laugh added, "Not sure I could live with myself if I didn't try to keep that fool kid from getting slaughtered."

Grant grinned as Nelly snorted, shaking her head.

"Are you agreeing I'm a fool, or something else?"

The horse just continued forward. After about two miles Grant pulled up, listening to the night sounds.

A slight breeze was blowing from the west, and off to the left he heard the scurrying of a night creature. Nothing seemed out of place. If anyone was hiding here, they'd been here long enough for the night to accept them.

Nelly tugged at the reins, stomping her hoof. "Okay, let's move on then," giving the horse a slight bump in the ribs, moving ahead at a slow walk. Grant was anxious to find the kid, but to ride without taking the time to listen and check the terrain, he could easily miss something that Boggs would overlook. This of course was dependent on the kid being savvy about hiding.

So far, he'd stayed on the trail. Grant's instinct was that the young man was not familiar with the area, so he'd probably keep to the trail as long as he could.

The farther Grant rode, the more the shadows of the past haunted him. When the moon finally started to rise, Grant almost shouted in relief. The rock formations off to his right rose like headstones in a cemetery. "Enough of this," he groused as the past continued beating at him.

He needed to focus on looking for any kind of trail he could find. He was far enough away from civilization that any tracks he found were most likely to be what he was looking for.

Dismounting, he struck a match. Bending low, he checked the ground. He cursed himself for not taking the time to look at the tracks that had been around the saloon. To do so would have helped him figure out which tracks were that of the kid and those of the crowd with Boggs.

"Some great tracker you are, overlooking something so simple," he said as the match burned down. At least he had an idea of those who had passed this way.

Continuing on, Grant traveled by instinct. As it was, he almost missed the small side trail. It was his horse that alerted him.

Dismounting, Grant struck another match. A lone rider had turned off while the bulk of the tracks continued on. He paused. It might be the young man, or just someone heading home. If he followed the lone rider and it was a mistake, the young man could die.

"Just choose," he told himself. Remounting, Grant turned onto the side trail.

# CHAPTER
## Four

Hetty kept Odysseus running for as long as she dared. Finally she knew she needed to slow down, not only for Odysseus, but for herself. She didn't know the country. The ground was becoming more uneven. Should they happen to plunge into a gully, or hole in the road, she and her horse would be done for.

Hetty's heart was pounding so loud, she couldn't hear anything else. Halting Odysseus after guiding him behind a slight lift in the ground, Hetty strove to slow her breathing. Taking a final deep breath, Hetty almost succeeded in calming herself when she caught the sound of hoof beats coming from behind her. It might just be a coincidence, but Hetty didn't think that was the case. From the sound, it might be anywhere from five to eight horses rapidly approaching.

"Well Odysseus, it looks like a long night," Hetty said leaning over to pat the horse's neck. "Think we might be able to shake them if we can find someplace off the trail. Seems I remember an area a short ways back," she continued as she reined around to head back the way she'd come. "Let's hope it's there and we reach it before the crowd gets here."

Hetty knew she was taking a big chance heading back toward the oncoming riders, but it seemed the only way to buy herself some more time. About a quarter of a mile she found a trail that led off to the side. Turning Odysseus, she'd gone a short distance when the riders thundered by. Letting out the breath she had been holding, she continued on as quietly as possible. With luck she'd be a long way off before those chasing her knew she'd turned off.

"Who knew Conover Boggs would be this far west, Odysseus? I thought he would still be in prison." Hetty sighed. "At least I was able contact Harrison's brother." Hetty smiled, remembering the startled look on Grant's face. If she hadn't known, she would have believed him to be the man who'd fallen through the schoolroom door, to collapse at her feet. The difference of course, Grant was bearded and covered with trail dirt. Harrison had been clean shaven and well dressed, with the exception of the blood on his clothing from the gunshot. If Harrison had not been so insistent, Hetty would have stayed to find out why he had been shot.

Right on the heels of her memories was the knowledge that she'd told Grant to meet her outside. How was she going to get the letter to him now? Did she dare head back to the saloon? Would he even be there?

Stars glittered in the velvet night, what moon there was seemed to be playing hide and seek with the clouds. The day had been warm, but the nights quickly cooled off on the high plains of Colorado. Hetty barely noticed, so focused was she on getting to safety, the problem of Conover Boggs, and finding Grant. Hetty pulled up, listening, just in case the pursuing riders had caught on. All was quiet, and Hetty sighed with relief.

She still couldn't understand Boggs being here. She'd run him down that day when he'd shot Mr. Jenkins, the mercantile owner. Because of her age, she'd not had to face Boggs in the courtroom. That had been about ten years ago.

She still remembered everything so clearly after all this time. She'd been riding into town, and despite her mother's attempts to get her into a dress, at twelve she was still wearing trousers. The locals were used to her, but there were many a stranger who thought she was a boy. She'd just turned the corner when Boggs came out of the mercantile, Mr. Jenkins walking out after him. Boggs had turned and shot him. The sheriff had run out at the sound of the shot. As he was preparing to fire, Bogs turned and fired at the sheriff.

The sheriff, who'd always been kind to her, hit the dirt. Without thinking, she had kicked Bess in the ribs and the old horse had jumped into a run, hitting Boggs. The hit knocked him down, sending his pistol flying. The sheriff, who was unhurt, fired, hitting Boggs in the leg. When Hetty rode back and told sheriff Watkins what she'd seen, Boggs threatened to kill her. She'd breathed a sigh of relief when he'd been sentenced to life in prison.

Now, here he was, and after her. If she could get back to Kiowa Wells and into a dress, it might be enough to keep her safe, since he must still think she was that boy. Of course that was at least two days away and she wasn't sure where she was.

With a sigh, Hetty continued away from Pueblo. Taking a sighting from the stars, Hetty realized she was heading south. Turning to the left, using what cover she could, she began her journey home, back to her students. She missed them, but had to admit until Boggs showed up, she'd enjoyed wearing pants and the freedom they gave her. For now she was safe, she hoped. Once back home, she would try to find another way to contact Grant and deliver the letter.

"Odysseus, we've had an adventure, and I liked it. Now, however, it's time to go home. I'm going to trust you to keep quiet so we can get out of here." She hoped by talking she might stay awake, but as the adrenaline wore off, Hetty found herself dozing. Jerking herself awake, she pulled Odysseus to a halt.

"Think I need to walk a bit, and give you a rest," she said patting the horse's neck. Throwing her leg over to dismount, she felt her grip begin to slip. She grabbed the saddle horn, but lost her grip. Hetty flipped backward and as she fell, her left foot remained in the stirrup. "Stay still boy," she ordered Odysseus, as she struggled to pull her foot loose. From her position, she couldn't quite get up high enough to reach her foot. On her right was a rock. "Head to the rock, boy," she told the horse.

Slowly Odysseus walked over, gently dragging Hetty with him. Hetty was working to lever herself up on the rock when she noticed a lone horse heading her way.

"Now what?" Hetty murmured as she relaxed, feigning unconsciousness. She prayed Odysseus would stand quiet. With the dark, perhaps the person wouldn't notice and move on. Out of the slit in her eyes, Hetty saw a horse with a man in the saddle. His face was hidden. The moon chose that moment to disappear behind a cloud. She saw he'd seen her and Odysseus. Hetty tensed, fearing the worst.

Taking stock of her surroundings, Hetty searched for a way to defend herself without firing the pistol. To shoot would only compound her circumstances. The noise would bring notice by the very people she was trying to avoid. At the same time, perhaps the person was just riding to somewhere close by. Perhaps they were just stopping to help.

Hetty heard the man sigh as he pulled up. "What do we have here?" she heard him say as he dismounted and moved over to where she lay.

"Wonder if this is the 'polecat' that Con is looking for?"

he said as he released Hetty's foot.

Hetty tensed at his words. When he leaned down to check on her she threw a handful of dirt in his eyes, grabbing a rock in her fist.

"What the..." Hetty heard as she tried to rise, only to stumble back. Catching herself, Hetty straightened, moving forward, rock steady in her hand.

# CHAPTER
*Five*

O ne moment Grant was standing over a prone body, the next found him clawing at his eyes trying to get the dirt out of them.

"What the…?" he growled, shaking his head as he heard footsteps rushing toward him. Through blurry eyes, he saw someone with a raised hand rushing toward him. He barely had time to duck as a hand holding a rock rushed by his head. As the assailant ran past, Grant put out an arm, grabbing the person around the waist. He felt, rather than saw, an arm swing back. He barely avoided being hit again. Instead, the blow landed on his left shoulder. With an effort, Grant maintained his hold, but just barely.

"Stop fighting and behave," Grant told his assailant, "I'm trying to help you."

"By turning me over to Conover Boggs?" Hetty spat out, forgetting to lower her voice in her agitation.

"Not if I can help it," Grant replied. He strengthened

his grip as he heard the sound of horses coming their way.

"Then," Hetty began, only to have a hand cover her mouth before she could say any more.

Out of the darkness the approaching horses halted close by. One moved closer just as the moon decided to make an appearance.

"Well, Grant, see you caught the boy. Nice work," Con said, grinning as he stepped off his horse. "Now young man," Con continued, moving toward the two.

Grant felt Hetty tense. Hoping his instincts were correct, he stopped Boggs with his next words. With his hand still over Hetty's mouth, he interrupted, "Slight mistake there, Con, this is my wife."

Grant felt Hetty stiffen. It was while holding her, he realized it wasn't some young boy, but a woman. Whatever else he might be, he would never let a woman get into the hands of someone like Boggs.

"Wife? What kind of game you playin'?" Con asked, his eyes glittering with anger. He pulled his pistol, his hand unsteady in his rage.

"No game," Grant replied, then leaned in closer, kissing Hetty's cheek, his hand still over her mouth. His lips moved to her ear as he whispered, "Just play along and you may live another day."

"My wife," Grant said again turning Hetty toward him. He replaced his hand with his lips. The moonlight gave Grant a closer look at the woman's face. He could see fear, confusion and determination all at once in the eyes staring at him. The next thing he knew, arms were snaking around his neck and a body molding itself to his contours.

"You can call me Hetty," she whispered in his ear as they broke the kiss.

"Seems there's something else going on here," Grant heard as he tried to catch his breath. His instincts had saved him again, but now what would happen? He really didn't want to have a woman along, but he couldn't let Con have her. Still, that kiss stunned him. So stunned he almost missed Con's next words.

"Can you prove it?"

"You don't believe…" Grant started.

"I've waited a long time for this polecat," Con interrupted.

While Grant was crossing words with Con, Hetty had been fumbling with something around her neck. She hadn't tried to run and Grant felt there she had some common sense. Of course, when he thought about it, running around in men's clothing wasn't the wisest thing to do.

"Here," Hetty held out a locket. "He gave me this, but when I found out what he was, I couldn't stay with him."

Con lit a match, and opening the locket saw the engraving. "What's this I Corinthians 13:13?"

Before Hetty could respond, Grant answered as he placed her hand on his heart. "The greatest of these is love."

Hetty was surprised at Grant and his knowledge of that verse. She was even more astounded when, without a word, Con returned the locket. Grant helped Hetty fasten it around her neck. He was grateful for Hetty's quick thinking. Taking Hetty's hand, Grant said, "Well, if you don't mind, I'm going to take my errant wife and..."

"Not so fast," Con interrupted. "I think it might be best if we traveled together. We can help you hang onto that wife of yours."

Grant could hear the maliciousness in Con's voice. He also felt Hetty tense, saw her hand inch toward her pistol. Putting his hand close to Hetty's moving hand, Grant queried, "You want us to ride with you? In case you hadn't been listening that's why she left."

Con, and those riding with him started laughing. It wasn't a pleasant sound, and Grant couldn't imagine what that sound meant to Hetty. He felt her try to break away from him. He felt her reaching for the pistol again.

Con must have seen the action for he laughed. "Well,

friend Grant, glad you kept your wife from shooting someone. That would've been unwise."

"If I get a chance," Hetty began, stepping back a step as Con moved over. He raised a hand to strike, but something stopped him.

Glaring first at Grant, then Hetty, Con snarled, "Keep an eye on her. I'm doing you a favor. If she left cause you was an outlaw, well, we'll just have to make her one, too."

Grant, who'd started to move as Con raised his hand, countered, "Don't know that she would go for that. But you're right, I'd like to keep her around."

Hetty turned in surprise, opening her mouth to speak, but instead closed it as she glared at those around them.

With little choice, Grant and Hetty mounted up. They were soon closed in on all sides. Con had let them know that the two were not to leave. The consensus seemed to be that Grant's wife would take off the first chance she had. Sensing the truth of that, Grant moved in close on the pretense of giving her a hug. As he pulled her in close he whispered, "Patience, I need to get out of here, too."

She turned toward him returning the fake hug. "Why?"

He was about to answer when one of the men rode up placing a hand on her shoulder. Grant started his horse toward the man, but stopped when he heard, "Where did you find that vest? It's mighty nice."

Shaking her shoulder, the man returned his hand to his side as she answered, "Back in St. Joe. Bought the boots there, too."

"Were you planning on running away then?"

Grant held his breath, a false word now would be a disaster.

"No, I planned on sending the vest back to my father, but word came that he died so I kept it," Hetty replied, her voice sincere but sad. "The shoes I bought for me. I wasn't sure what I might run into after crossing the river. Besides, we weren't married yet."

Grant relaxed tense shoulders, letting his breath out in

relief. This fake wife was turning out to be more than he'd ever thought. Problem was, they both needed to get away. He needed to continue his search, but he still wasn't clear why this woman said she had something from Harrison. Why had she dressed in men's clothing to pass on a message, and what was that message? Now was not the place to find out. The biggest question was why Con was so sure she was the person who'd...who'd what?

Moving closer again, Grant studied this strange woman, trying to puzzle things out. Having no luck, Grant grinned and speaking loud enough so the others could hear, "Dear are you still angry?

Hetty didn't answer, just glared. Those around laughed.

Grant leaned over, pulling Hetty into a kiss. He prayed she wouldn't knock him off his horse Nelly. Even so, the slap hurt, but he kissed her anyway, then whispered "How did you know who I was?"

The glare Grant received shocked him. Was it for the question or the kiss he wondered. He moved away from Hetty as the men laughed even louder.

"You sure you want to stay married to that wildcat?" Con asked.

While the others laughed, Grant understood the meaning underneath Con's words.

# CHAPTER
## Six

S o this was *Grant, the man she'd left Kiowa Wells to find,* Hetty thought, glancing over to the man riding beside her. His kissing her took her by surprise; in fact, it embarrassed her. She'd never been kissed, never believed it would happen. She was even more chagrined at her actions during the kiss. Her mind whirled at the situation she was now in.

Hetty decided it best to play along, watching and hoping for a chance to escape. She would take that chance alone or with Grant, but escape she must. Why had Grant decided to surrender, to not fight their way out? She would have taken off the minute the others showed up, but Grant stopped her with a steel grip, one she couldn't break.

She wondered what the connection between Grant and Conover Boggs could be. She knew Grant had the label of outlaw, yet, somehow it didn't fit him. He also wasn't acting like she'd imagined when she began this journey. Looking back, she really knew very little; only that Harrison was adamant about Grant getting the letter. Of course, now she had no way of passing it on without blowing their cover.

Hetty wondered if she had made a huge mistake. To her, delivering the letter was a simple thing to do. She'd promised to find Grant and deliver the letter. Instead she'd let her imagination get the upper hand. Now, she and Grant were virtual prisoners, but not to the casual observer.

Boggs rode on through the night with no break. Hetty found herself dozing off. In her dreams she could imagine herself being held by someone who would comfort her in this situation she found herself. "You have no one to blame but yourself," she muttered in her sleep.

Jerking awake, Hetty thought, *My parents were right. I'm destined to live my life alone.* Somehow that idea hurt more than it had in the past. She glanced at Grant, blushing at how they had kissed. She was grateful for the dark and how it hid her shame from everyone else.

Hetty dozed again, only to have warmth hit her face, waking her. Then she realized the angle felt wrong. She began to straighten, finding herself unable to move. In a panic, she tensed, a scream forming, but cut short with a hand over her mouth.

"Relax, I won't let anything happen to you."

Hetty's eyes popped open. Green eyes greeted her brown ones.

"Feel like returning to your own horse?"

Hetty relaxed. If she were honest, she wanted to remain where she was. She wanted to enjoy being held, being cared for. Then common sense took over. She sat up. "Probably would be a good idea." She felt heat move up her face when Grant didn't immediately let her go.

"Hold up," Grant yelled. "I think my wife would like to return to her own mount."

Grant's words were met with snickering laughter, bringing even more color to Hetty's face. But they stopped moving as Hetty resumed her seat on Odysseus.

"Sorry," she whispered to Grant. He simply grinned as he helped her onto her horse.

Hetty felt the whole situation was becoming more convoluted. As they continued moving west and into the foothills, Hetty began to worry. Would they continue upward into the mountains? She shivered. If Boggs wanted to get rid of her, the mountains would be the perfect place. The chance of her body ever being found was slim. Then she looked over at Grant, who seemed totally at ease. Would he continue to be the hero?

As they continued westward, Hetty wondered if Grant noticed they were utilizing their surroundings to stay hidden from anyone who might be following. She knew Boggs must be wanted, why were all the others following blindly? Were they of the same ilk as Boggs? The thought made her feel faint.

"Any idea where we're heading?" Hetty asked Grant.

"This area used to be an outlaw's hideout. There's a town somewhere nearby. I've heard of it, but never been there. Last I heard, the place was now populated by some pretty decent people."

As they moved into a meadow, a lovely place and a relief from the rocky terrain they had been traveling, Boggs shouted from the front, "Going to visit some relatives." Then he laughed as if it were some kind of joke. "If you know what's good for you, you'll play along, or better yet, just keep your mouth shut no matter what happens."

The sun had risen over the mountains casting a pleasant glow over the green valley. To Hetty, it was a comforting sight after the darkness they'd been riding through.

Hetty took a moment, when she thought no one was looking, to readjust her binding. She glanced over at Grant, then quickly looked away. His face had taken on a harshness that frightened her. Was she the cause of such dark thoughts? Somehow the thought made her tear up.

"Be careful," Grant hissed at her.

"I am careful," she retorted just as quietly. She turned away, stung at his remark. Just as quickly, she realized none of her actions so far gave any proof to her being careful. But then why should she care what Grant or anyone else thought? Once she made it through all this, she would never see him or any of these people again. On the heels of that thought came concern for Harrison. Was he healing or had he taken a turn for the worst?

Hetty heard Grant snort, but when she turned back, she saw he was smiling.

"Well, I'm usually careful." Then taking the plunge, she asked, "Why haven't you asked me what I wanted to see you about, or even how I knew your brother?"

The change in Grant was instantaneous. The look in his eyes frightened her. She quickly added, "Not that it's any of my business."

"You're right, it's not," he growled.

# CHAPTER
*Seven*

G rant glanced over at Hetty. This woman was a source of surprise to him. She was also a strong woman like his mother. No, not like his mother. Grant felt that Hetty was strong in spite of her fear. To him, his mother seemed strong because of her fear.

When Hetty had begun to fall from her horse, Grant caught her, placing her in front of him on Nelly. Those around them snickered, making lewd comments. But Grant ignored them. Instead he focused on the woman in his arms. Looking at her, in the dim starry light, he thought she was striking. Not a beauty in the accepted sense, but there was something compelling about her. He felt a sense of peace as he held her. When she mumbled, he smiled. He didn't want to let her go.

When Hetty first opened her eyes, he caught the unguarded sweetness there. That sweetness quickly turned to confusion, then understanding.

He called a halt despite incurring Boggs' wrath, and

helped Hetty return to her own mount. As he swung into his saddle, he felt empty without her in front of him.

They had ridden just a short distance when Hetty asked a question that brought back all the pain and frustration of his childhood. His eyes had lashed out in anger, although he had said nothing. He saw her flinch, but so strong was his reaction he couldn't pull away from it quickly enough. She'd been contrite, but his anger cut off any further conversation. It was at that moment Boggs decided to acknowledge their presence again.

"What kind of lovey-dovey stuff you whisperin' about?" Boggs demanded. "I warned you about behavin'. I still ain't sure you two are on the level."

Hetty opened her mouth to retort, but Grant placed a hand on her arm, squeezing it as a warning. She squared her shoulders, taking a deep breath before glaring at Boggs.

Seeing Hetty's reaction, and Grant's response, Boggs started laughing, although his words were no veiled threat. "Control that woman of yours, Davis, or I'll take her off your hands."

"I might let you," Grant began, then looking over at Hetty, he smiled, "No, I went to all this trouble to find and get her back, I think I'll keep her."

"So you think you'll keep me?" Hetty challenged. "What if I don't..."

"Now dear," Grant interrupted, grinning widely. If they weren't in this situation, Grant thought he might really like to get to know Hetty. One thing was certain, she was never boring. He didn't know from one minute to the next what she might do. He only prayed she'd do nothing to get herself killed.

Despite wanting to argue, Hetty realized the situation was fraught with danger. She wanted to live, to get back to her life. At the same time, a part of her was enjoying the part she was playing as Grant's wife. Not only was he protective, but he was kind, doing what he could to make sure she was comfortable, safe. Of course, this farce would never be real. Her parents' words came roaring back. She tried to shut them out with Grandmams' words, but it was no use. She felt the familiar pain in her heart.

"'Bout time you put some control on."

Whatever Boggs was going to say was cut short as Hetty jumped from Odysseus and into Boggs. Her actions caught everyone off guard and down Boggs went with Hetty pounding at his face and neck.

"I've had enough," Boggs roared. This time his words were accompanied by a violent backhand slap. Hetty's eyes watered and blood started from her bottom lip where it had crushed against her teeth.

The next instant she was grabbed from behind, effectively ending her assault on the big man.

"Calm down," Hetty heard Grant say, but once started, there seemed to be no stopping her. Hetty turned, raising her fist to break Grant's hold. The concern and fear in Grant's eyes halted her assault. Hetty's anger faded as she took a gulp of air to regain control.

"I'm fine. You can let me go," Hetty told Grant as she wiped her blood from her lip, with the kerchief Grant handed her. She could feel him shaking as he continued to stand between her and Boggs.

"Davis, wife or no wife, that she-cat is not going to attack anyone again. Hank, tie her to her horse."

Grant started to intercede, but Boggs said, "Don't try to stop me or you'll be one dead husband."

About two miles farther on, Boggs called a halt.

"Tie her to that tree over there. I'll deal with her when I get back," Boggs ordered.

Grant moved forward, but he was grabbed by two of the others and Hetty was dragged away.

Shoulders slumped, she barely felt the ropes or heard Hank's words, "Don't worry, if all goes well, he'll get over it."

Leaning back against the tree, Hetty searched her mind

for ways to keep herself together. Finally her temper had gotten her into a situation she probably wouldn't get out of. To add to her guilt, she had involved Grant.

An hour later, she remembered Hank's words as he'd secured her to the tree. What had Hank meant with his words? What would happen if Boggs didn't get over it? Would he take it out on Grant too? She looked out at the sky and the world around her. What was she going to do, what was going to happen to Grant, what was Boggs going to do when he returned?

# CHAPTER
*Eight*

I t was late afternoon when Boggs returned from town. With him was another gentleman, who was grinning from ear to ear.

Boggs went over to Grant, but Hetty couldn't hear what was being said. Grant was arguing, but he was not winning. It was when Grant nodded that Hetty heard Boggs call, "Bring the bride over."

*Bride?* Hetty thought. Then Hank was untying her. He escorted her to where Grant was stiffly standing before Boggs and the other man.

At Hetty's approach, Boggs started rubbing his hands together, a chilling grin on his face. "I still don't trust you two, but I wanted to do something special. This here is the preacher from town, he's going to re-marry you two."

Fire started in Hetty's eyes, her body tensed as she tried to break free from Hank, but before she'd made three steps, an arm around whipped around her waist and pulled her back. The men around started laughing.

"Seems your wife don't like the idea of being married to

you, Davis." Boggs' voice shook with laughter.

Hetty started to answer, but instead closed her lips. She turned, glaring at Hank for pulling her back.

"This is what comes from trying to help someone," she mumbled to herself, fear and excitement warring within her at the thought of this farce of a marriage. Still, the adventurer side of her decided that once done, she would be married, something she never expected. Of course, if they got out of this, she'd let Grant go his way, and wouldn't fight a divorce.

"What?" Grant said in a tight voice.

Hetty turned her head and saw the question in his eyes. As much as she needed a friend right now, he didn't deserve what was happening.

"Nothing," she responded, "sorry," she continued, hoping he understood she wasn't angry, just scared and confused.

Grant moved over to Hetty, pulling her close, whispering. "You don't have a husband somewhere do you?"

"No, do you have a wife hidden away?" Hetty responded in the same soft whisper.

The question relaxed Hetty. *Leave it to an outlaw to think about breaking the law*, Hetty thought, grateful for Grant and his easy way. *Of course he's probably not happy about the situation either.*

The whole event was unreal, with Grant and Hetty saying vows, signing papers with two of the outlaws as witnesses. When the circus was over, the crowd chanted over and over, "Kiss her like you mean it, make her toe the line."

Grant could see Hetty was embarrassed and upset with the men and the whole situation. Leaning in, he pulled her close. "Up for another round?" he softly asked. At her slight nod, Grant pulled her in for a kiss. Again Hetty returned his kiss, and left Grant breathless.

"All I can say is, whoever taught you to kiss..." Grant

began in Hetty's ear, only to have her reply, "You are the first person I've ever kissed."

Once her confession was made, Hetty turned red, averting her face in shame. Grant gently turned her to face him once more. "You've nothing to be ashamed of. Your kisses have been the sweetest I've ever had."

The next thing Grant and Hetty knew, Boggs was between them, and started questioning Hetty.

"Now that we've got that taken care of, why'd you run out of the bar?" Boggs, his hand grabbing Hetty's shirt and pulling her close.

Grant grabbed Boggs, intent on making him let go of Hetty, but the others pulled him away.

"I ran," Hetty replied, quietly dropping a bombshell, "because I saw you looking at me and I wanted to get away. Just as I was almost out the door, *this man*—my husband—shows up. In some ways, he's just as bad as you."

"You couldn't tell by the way you was kissin' him," Boggs sneered.

Hetty squirmed from the man's grasp, saying, "That doesn't mean I can't enjoy a kiss now and then. He is good at that."

Before she could say more, Grant grabbed her. "You're right, you were a fool, but I'd no complaints at the time, or now," Grant said as he grabbed Hetty around the waist. "I'd been hunting you for some time, and now that you're here, we can move along," Grant declared to Hetty. "And *you* will kindly stop man-handling my wife," Grant snarled at Boggs.

Whirling, despite the surprise of being grabbed, Hetty slipped Grant's hold and ran back toward Boggs, intent on breaking his nose. Before she made two steps, Grant tackled her to the ground.

"If you're smart, my fire-eating wife, you'll act like I've subdued you, perhaps knocked you out," Grant whispered throwing a punch to her head.

Hetty stiffened, then relaxed realizing the punch Grant threw had no power. She decided to play along, see what happened.

Hetty heard Grant move away. "Sorry, that's one thing I love about my wife, you never know what she's going to do, but you've no right to treat her the way you did, that's my job."

"Damn she's got spunk," Boggs commented. "Good luck bein' married to that one."

Hetty wanted to smile, but that didn't last long. The next words made her want to roll over and run.

"But spunk and guts won't save her or you if I find you've been lying to me," he growled. "We'll rest a bit, then we got some miles to put behind us. Hank, take her back to the tree and tie her up again, don't want her attacking anyone," Boggs ordered.

"Davis, tell me more about this wife of yours," Boggs ordered, his arm going around Grant's shoulder, pulling him in the opposite direction.

Grant wanted to go to Hetty, keep her safe, but they needed to be careful until they could get away.

# CHAPTER
*Nine*

H etty woke, feeling someone working on the ropes behind her. Then strong arms lifted her. She started to stiffen as a hand came over her mouth. "Quiet, don't make a sound," sounded in her ear. Still groggy from sleep, she couldn't tell who was speaking. She was thrown over a shoulder as the man walked away from the camp. Her head banged against the man's back. The rush of blood to her head had Hetty fighting to keep herself from retching. Just when she felt she could hold on no longer she was placed gently on the ground.

Hetty lay still, trying to think her way out of this mess. She was so focused she didn't hear Grant speak. "What?"

"Shhhh," Grant whispered into her ear. "Nice work, you're doing okay." Grant picked her up carrying her farther away. "but we're not out of the woods yet," he finished.

"So, what do you think you're doing?" Hetty snarled

quietly, hoping there was no one nearby to hear. "Did Boggs set this up?" She knew she was being unreasonable, but the words couldn't be stopped.

"No, just know Boggs is pure poison if you get on the wrong side of him," Grant answered. "We need to get out of here. It might be easier to stay with him, but I think in the long run, that would be a mistake. Of course, it helped that he knew I'd been in prison."

Shaking her head to clear it, Hetty said, "Prison?" Then Hetty remembered Will saying Grant had been in prison, but his actions, his kindness had confused her. She'd just wanted to deliver Harry's letter, let Grant know what happened and then head back home. Now she found herself married, and she was going to need all her wits, which were a bit rattled, to get herself out of this mess. Perhaps she could give him the letter now, and they could just go their separate ways. His next words squashed that idea.

"It will probably be safer for both of us to travel together until we get away. While Boggs told me what I needed to know, you wouldn't be safe by yourself. Boggs seems to want you dead for some reason. I think there's something you're not telling me."

To change the subject, Hetty said, "I almost lost my stomach on the back of your shirt."

Grant grinned. "I'm glad you didn't."

To cover her embarrassment Hetty started talking. "My father always said charm would only get you so far. After that, well, he never finished." Hetty sighed. "I took it to mean you had to be more than what people saw."

Grant stared at her and Hetty felt trepidation. He grinned, "Are you saying I'm charming? I'll take the compliment, but we still have some things to talk about."

He was being too observant, and charming. She turned her head. She was in enough trouble already thanks to him, and his smile was hard to resist. Now, they needed to focus on getting away.

Grant turned Hetty's face toward him. "We'll talk later, when we get away."

Hetty felt her cheeks reddening. She held on to her temper and clamped her lips shut. Grant's words reinforced her feeling of being trapped. Her mouth wasn't creating saliva, she felt her heart would escape her chest at any moment. She forced herself to look him in the eye, bringing as much confidence into the look she gave him. Hetty could hear the laughter from the camp and wondered how long before someone realized they were gone?

Grant exhaled, his hands supporting Hetty's chin. "This isn't over," he smiled. "Stay here, I'll be back."

Hetty wanted to ask where he was going, but she felt if she questioned his actions, Grant would think less of her. Hetty heard his chuckle as he walked away. She saw him moving around the edge of the fire, avoiding the men celebrating there. When one called to him, he nodded, but kept on moving.

Hetty, crept back to where she'd been tied to the tree and with some brush and limbs, created what she hoped would look like someone sleeping there. It wouldn't fool anyone who came close, but perhaps it would give them a bit more time if someone glanced that way to check on her.

Hetty had just returned to where Grant had left her when he returned. "I needed to get your saddlebags and some supplies."

Hetty nodded, telling him what she had done by the tree.

"Good idea, now let's get out of here.

Our horses are over on the far side," Grant whispered, holding Hetty steady.

Hetty followed Grant's lead. She was feeling a bit dizzy, but continued on. She then realized she couldn't walk straight. Calling over to Grant, "I need some..."

Grant hurried back as she started to fall. He swept her

up in his arms, carrying her over to Odysseus. "Are you sure you can ride?"

"Let's just get out of here," Hetty whispered back.

# CHAPTER
*Ten*

O nce Grant and Hetty had exited the hidden valley, they did their best to confuse their tracks, hoping to delay any pursuit that might be mounted to find them. First they rode through a sandy patch, then they doubled back, creating a confusion of tracks and directions. They weren't sure it would work, since it was still fairly dark.

Once the sun rose, they made better time, and were able to hide their tracks better. It was as they were coming out of the trees that Grant's horse shied, almost unseating him. Hetty looked over to see a large snake slithering away in the grass.

Hetty watched as Grant got Nelly under control, then asked, "You okay?"

A painful grin creased Grant's face. "I'll survive. Why didn't your horse react?"

"Odysseus was probably too far away. I also raised him

from a colt, so he tends to be calm. The only time he acts up is if someone else tries to ride him."

Grant nodded his acknowledgment then he indicated a faint trail leading off to the right, while a better one forked off to the left. "They will hopefully think we are heading back to civilization. Maybe we can get some time and distance by doing the opposite."

"It might work," Hetty responded. The two rode down the better trail, then cutting off, hit the smaller trail by cutting through the trees.

Although they were now legally married, Hetty was uncomfortable. She felt Grant was probably unhappy having a wife, although he'd not said anything about it. In truth, Hetty was glad he was doing his best to get them both to some kind of safety.

"Grant," Hetty began, getting her new husband's attention.

He looked over as she continued, "If you want, we can get a—"

"Let's talk about that later, "he growled. "Right now, we need to get beyond Boggs' reach."

"But, I don't want…"

"We'll talk later!"

Hetty looked away. As usual, she was causing problems. It seemed the only place she was competent and useful was in the classroom.

*Why did she have to have her adventure?* she wondered.

Continuing on, the two climbed upward, then down into valleys. Hour after hour they journeyed onward, the silence growing with each mile. The sun marked their time on its journey east to west. They had not seen anything of Boggs or any of his men, indicating they hadn't caught on to their escape any earlier than expected. Turning north had proved to be a wise move.

Hetty was getting tired despite the stops made to stretch and give the horses a rest. They were heading into another meadow when a butterfly landed briefly on her left hand. She admired its delicate beauty, the varied shades of yellow on its wings, before it flew off. She sighed, stretching to release the tension in her shoulders.

They rode into the trees, and finding a clearing, Grant felt a small fire and warm food would be okay. They both began gathering wood, and soon had the fire going. Finally, Hetty dug into her saddlebags, pulling out the letter.

"Grant," Hetty began, "this is the reason I was looking for you." She had been hesitant to broach the subject, but with all that had happened because of it, she felt it was time to hand it over.

Grant took the extended envelope and one he glanced at the writing, frowned, saying, "It doesn't matter, I have other, more important things to do."

"But aren't you…"

"No," he interrupted. He sat there, occasionally feeding the dying flames, saying nothing. "This is how much I care," Grant growled, tossing the letter toward the fire as he rose and walked away.

So shocked by his actions, Hetty barely made it to the fire in time to pull the letter from the flames. "You may not care, but I do. I would give almost anything to have someone care enough to contact me. I'd always dreamed someone would care enough to wonder if I was okay," Hetty said to the empty night that surrounded them. She replaced the letter in her saddlebags, then let the tears flow, not only for herself, but for Grant.

To Hetty, it seemed Grant didn't even care about his brother, his family. She didn't know if Grant's brother Harrison was alive. The one thing she knew, his arriving at her door had offered her the chance to step out of her ordinary day-to-day life. It wasn't that she'd been unhappy, in fact the opposite was true. Still, even with all that, this adventure, if she survived, was a memory that would carry her through the cold nights of her lonely old age.

When Grant returned, Hetty wanted to ask why he felt the way he did, but after his reaction with the letter, she decided to suppress her questions. Instead, to perhaps break the awkward silence, she inquired, "You said you were looking for someone. Since we know it wasn't me, despite what you told Boggs, may I ask, who is so important you put yourself in harm's way to find?"

Grant continued his silence, his eyes averted from the flames. Hetty turned when he didn't respond, and began preparing herself a place to sleep.

As she stretched out on the ground, she turned, catching a glimpse of Grant's profile. If she didn't know better, she would swear he was a stone statue. With a sigh, she pulled her blanket to her shoulders and turned her gaze to the night sky. "I always loved Homer's *Odyssey*," Hetty said, smiling at the memory of herself sitting under the tree, living the adventure in her mind. She wondered now what people would say about her relating to the hero instead of the long-suffering wife. She looked up, hoping Grant would say something. His silence was disturbing.

"And how do you think he would be as an old man, confined by age, to living within his four walls?" Grant asked, casting his eyes toward Hetty.

"Never thought about it," Hetty responded. "I imagine he would still be a vital person. I don't think he'd even be slowed down. It wasn't his nature. What about you?"

"What about me?"

"Who did, or do you admire?"

"My father," Grant said, then silence.

Hetty sighed and was almost asleep when Grant spoke. She wasn't sure if he was speaking to her or to himself so she remained silent.

"I found out early my mother hated me. She used to always say it was me, no matter who did something wrong. There were many switch beatings until I grew enough to fight back."

Grant was silent for a long time after that revelation.

Hetty could see him banking the fire and preparing his own sleeping spot. The stars shone down, and it seemed to Hetty those stars that fell were crying for the unhappy boy Grant must have been.

Hetty bowed her head, then looked up, a question on her lips. Grant's glance brooked no further questions. Her mind searched for a solution to his pain. From all she was learning, his life hadn't been easy. Still, nothing came to mind that might help.

Grant leaned back, closing his eyes, effectively stopping further conversation. Hetty was having none of that. "Why didn't you want to open the letter?" she asked.

"None of your concern," Grant answered, pulling his hat over his eyes, turning away from her.

Hetty squeezed her eyes shut, cutting off the tears that threatened. Rising, she moved over to the horses, leaning against Odysseus. She threw her arms around his neck. He'd been her refuge since she'd purchased him as a colt, despite her family's objections. No matter what happened in her life, Odysseus was her rock. "Seems I just can't get it right. Try to help someone, but..." Hetty stopped. There was a noise behind her. She'd been a fool to leave the fire, but Odysseus hadn't reacted.

# CHAPTER
*Eleven*

H etty felt a hand on her shoulder. She stiffened, preparing to strike or run when she heard Grant's voice.

"We'd lost our step-brother, Washington, early in the conflict between the states. My mother had been married before, but her husband died unexpectedly. Father treated Wash like his own son, and Mother didn't want Wash to join up." Grant paused, letting his hand fall from Hetty's shoulder.

"Mother became more manipulative, but no one else seemed to notice but me. We were pretty well off and folks just naturally catered to Mom. After Father's death, she turned her focus on my younger brother, Harry."

"I'm sorry, you don't..." Hetty began, but Grant continued on, ignoring or not hearing Hetty, so involved were his memories as they walked back to the fire.

"Harry and I, despite the eighteen months' difference

could have been twins. Many couldn't tell us apart. To Mother, Harry could do no wrong, even when he took to stealing, Mom always told everyone it was me. People believed her."

Hetty felt like she should stop Grant, but it seemed he needed to talk. She finally understood, or thought she did. But why would she have him sent to prison?

"Why would she..."

"I didn't want anything to do with her. I even tried to leave, but she framed me for rustling. I'd managed to escape for a time, but eventually I realized I couldn't keep running and turned myself in."

Hetty couldn't understand how a mother could do something like that. "Didn't people get suspicious?" she asked.

"Our family, especially my mother, knew how to manipulate people. I didn't have a chance, and Harry went along with her." The anger and hurt coming out in his voice, cut into Hetty's heart. She didn't know what to do, but she wanted to try to ease his pain, she just didn't know how.

"Of course, the minute I started fighting back, Mother used that as proof that I was bad. Even when my brother Harrison acted out, it was me who bore the brunt of the punishment. The only one who'd caught on and stood up for me was my father. I can't prove it, but I think she killed him, but not before he wrote the Will leaving everything to me." At Hetty's gasp, Grant paused, then continued, "I think she thought if I were in prison, Harrison would take over by pretending to be me. We looked enough alike, he could do it. Even if he couldn't pull off being me, there was always the chance I'd die in prison, or become the outlaw they say I am. No matter what happened, she would have everything."

Hetty started to go over and put her arms around Grant. The matter-of-fact way he told the story hurt her worse than if he'd shown anger. As Grant continued,

Hetty stayed where she was.

"I'm searching for a witness to her actions and who can clear me of all the false charges, including the rustling that sent me to prison."

Somehow 'I'm sorry' didn't seem adequate. Instead Hetty whispered, "I'll help in whatever way I can, if you let me. I can tell you when Harrison showed up at the school room door, he'd been shot. Dr. Josie didn't know if he would make it or not but she's…"

"I don't care," Grant growled.

The pain and finality Hetty heard in those three words broke her heart. She vowed she would do what she could to help Grant, whether he wanted it or not. Somehow the label of outlaw he had didn't hold up the more she learned about him, especially if what he said was true. The truth was, she wanted to believe him, believe in him, but then where did Harrison fit into all this?

Lying back on her saddle, Hetty closed her eyes and was soon asleep. It was during the night she felt chilled then was burning up. She wanted to tell Grant, but then he would probably take her into town. There was a chance that Boggs or one of his men would see them and then their escape would have been for nothing. Hetty fell asleep, once the episode passed.

# CHAPTER
*Twelve*

T he second day after they'd managed to give Boggs the slip, Grant and Hetty came up to the Arkansas River just above Canon City. Grant insisted they stay away from the town. "It's too close to Pueblo," he said. Hetty barely heard the "Plus I spent time at the territorial prison there."

"I'm sorry," she'd spoken before thinking, perhaps he'd not meant for her to hear that last part.

Grant didn't respond to Hetty's words. Instead he continued on across the river, then they began climbing, as they continued north.

Hetty was struggling to stay seated, the hot and cold of the night before sweeping through her. Grant glanced back in time to see her swaying, in danger of falling out of the saddle. He whirled, dismounting to catch her before she hit the ground.

Startled at the sudden stop, Hetty struggled to get loose

from the strong arms holding her.

Realizing Hetty was awake, Grant reluctantly set Hetty on her feet. He noted his reluctance to release her. He would have to think about that later. Right now, he was trying to calm Hetty.

"You were falling," Grant explained, then asked, "why didn't you say…"

"You've been in your own world since we crossed the river. It was as if you were in a different place," Hetty interrupted.

Grant began to make a heated reply, then let it go. He *had* been somewhere else. He was so close to one of the men he sought. He had forgotten Hetty and that thought bothered him more than he liked. "All I can say is sorry. You're right, I was focused on where I was headed."

Hetty appreciated him telling her the truth, but it hurt that he'd forgotten her.

"Why did you fight me?" Grant's question cut into her thoughts.

"You startled me," Hetty lied. She couldn't tell him her secret. She told no one about the time some of the neighborhood boys had pulled her off her horse and harassed her, tossing her from one to the other. Nothing had happened, but she'd been so embarrassed. She added, "I'm sorry you've been saddled with me."

Grant accepted her explanation for fighting him, but didn't know how to respond to her last statement. Instead he asked, "You feel up to traveling a few more miles? There's a place not too far from here where we can make camp."

"Sure, I'm all right now," Hetty answered. Suiting action to words, Hetty mounted up, calling to Grant, "Hurry up slowpoke."

Grinning with relief that Hetty appeared to be okay, Grant followed suit and the two set off again.

They rode in a comfortable silence through the afternoon. Grant thought to himself how lucky he was to have a traveling companion who didn't find it necessary to fill silences with words. Most women he'd known talked constantly, as if silence was a terrifying thing. Even his own mother, when berating him, would go on and on until he would try to escape. Of course, he learned that only set her off on another tirade. Eventually his father, while still alive, would rescue him, sending him off on some task that would take him away from the house. Oh, how he'd enjoyed that alone time.

Pulling up, he glanced back to find Hetty swaying in the saddle again. He started back as he watched her. Her face was pale, her eyes bright and feverish looking. How had he missed that earlier?

Hetty had been so focused on following Grant, hoping they would soon arrive at the place he spoke about, she didn't realize she was swaying in the saddle. When she realized what was happening, she grabbed the saddle horn in a death grip. Just as she thought she was okay, everything went blurry then black. She fell from Odysseus, cracking her head against a rock.

Grant heard Hetty's horse stop, glancing back he saw her on the ground. "Blasted woman, why didn't she say something?" he grumbled as he rode back.

All complaints left him when he saw blood spreading out from the rock under Hetty's head. Grant didn't remember dismounting as he rushed to Hetty's side, feeling for a pulse, and using his kerchief to try and stop the flow of blood, but nothing he did helped.

"Hetty, Harriet," Grant repeated over and over. Finally he heard a soft moan as Hetty moved her fingers. Letting go a sigh of relief, Grant continued working to revive Hetty. Kneeling on the gravel, Grant didn't notice the pain from the cuts to his knees.

Fearful of doing more harm, Grant knew he needed to get Hetty to help. Carefully, holding Hetty's head and neck as stable as possible, he carefully placed her in his saddle and worked to mount up behind her, without releasing his hold.

# CHAPTER
## Thirteen

G rant rode toward Canon City, the town he tried to avoid. He would just deal with whatever happened there. Hetty was more important.

An hour later, he came to a small cabin. "Hello the house?" Even when he called out, Hetty didn't respond. She was dead weight in his arms. If it weren't for the rise and fall of her chest, he'd have sworn she was dead.

A middle aged-looking woman came to the door. "What can I…" She began, then seeing Hetty she hurried forward. "What happened?"

"She fell from her horse and hit her head. She's still breathing, but…" Grant stopped, he didn't want to continue, didn't want to think what might happen. Taking a deep breath, Grant continued, "If I could leave her here while I go for a doctor?"

"Who is she?"

"My wife."

The woman nodded, heading to the door of the cabin. "Come on in. I'll have my boy go for the doctor, it'll be quicker."

Grant tried dismounting while he still held Hetty. He didn't want to let her go.

"Let me help. Know you want to hold on to her, but if you drop her..." the woman insisted.

Grant finally accepted the woman's help, but the minute his feet hit the ground he took Hetty back into his arms.

"Clover," the woman yelled, "you go get Doc Brown."

A boy, about twelve, came from around the house, climbed onto a mule, then took off.

"Follow me."

Grant carried Hetty into the house. It was small and dark inside. Grant started to back away, but the weight in his arms stopped him. The woman continued on, pulling a curtain aside and indicated a small cot. Carefully, Grant lowered Hetty to the cot, retaining a hold on her hand. He heard the woman splashing water into a pan.

"Here," she said as she handed Grant a clean cloth, "You can start cleanin' around the cut while I heat some water. Know Doc is gonna need it."

"Thank you," Grant said, taking the cloth and basin the woman held out to him. Carefully, he began cleaning the cut while gently removing the dirt and rocks from Hetty's hair. His hand shook, as he cursed himself for not paying attention. This was followed by anger at his mother, then women in general. Yet, to Grant, Hetty wasn't like his mother or other women.

"Hetty, Hetty," Grant whispered, "come back."

Grant remained by Hetty's side, occasionally talking to her, wiping her face. How long he sat there, Grant didn't know. He heard someone ride up. A prickling at the back of his neck made him glance toward the door. The color drained from his face as he reached for his pistol. He didn't want to leave Hetty, but the cabin was no place to have a shootout. He heard Boggs ask the woman, "The folks who rode these horses, where are they?"

"They just wandered in here, weren't no one riding 'em. Did notice blood on the saddles."

"You expect me to—"

"Believe what you want, that's the truth." The woman cut in.

Grant continued holding his breath, waiting to hear how Boggs would react.

Watching the interplay between the woman and Boggs, he thought how the day had started out with such promise. He and Hetty had forded the river and were well on their way to a family he knew in the high meadows north of here. He'd hoped they could give him a lead for a man named Swisher. He was one of the men he was looking for. Swisher had worked for the family when they'd lived next to his own family.

Although the Wileys had started to believe the lies his mother had spread about him, Grant hoped they would be willing to help him clear his name, once he told his side of the story.

"Well, how 'bout I take a look inside? They's criminals and dangerous," Boggs said, his words pulling Grant back to the present. Grant wondered how much of the conversation he'd missed? Cursing himself for letting his mind wonder, Grant braced himself for what might come next.

"Wouldn't advise it, sister's down with measles," Grant heard her say. "If'n I was you, I'd head out, seein' as both them saddles had blood on 'em."

"Maybe you're right, but if you're lyin'..." Con left, the threat hanging as he rode toward Odysseus and Nelly.

"I've no reason ta lie," Maude shouted after him.

With a growl, Boggs grabbed for the reins of the two horses. He paused when he saw the rifle in the woman's hands pull up and aim at his stomach.

"You'll leave them horses here."

Grant watched as Boggs struggled to get a handle on his temper. Only a fool would buck a cocked weapon. "Whatever you say," he snarled, then with a kick to his horse, Boggs took off.

Letting go of the breath he'd been holding, Grant walked back to check on Hetty.

Her breathing was shallow, her face even more pale than before. Feeling guilty, Grant leaned down to whisper, "I'm sorry."

The woman returned to the cabin, and began mixing something at the table. "You ain't no criminal, don't care what that man said. By the way, name's Maude. And you'd be?"

Grant looked at the woman who had taken them in and lied to a very dangerous man to keep them safe. He felt the best he could do would be to tell the truth. "My name's Grant Davis and this is my wife Harriet, Hetty. I also spent a little more than a year in prison," Grant told Maude; "guess that makes me a criminal."

"You do it?"

"Would you believe me if I said no?"

"Yes," Maude replied. "My Joe, he's there now. He ain't no criminal, but he shot that man what tried to hurt me."

"I'm sorry, and now we brought more trouble to you," Grant said. How had things gotten so out of hand? He needed to get to the high mountain meadow before they caught up with him again. If he was going to die, he wanted it to be with a clear name. He wanted to put to rest all the lies his mother was spreading about him, and keep Hetty from the embarrassment of having an outlaw for a husband.

"I've had trouble before. Here, now help me put some spots on yer lady."

At Grant's puzzled look, Maude smiled. "It's a trick I learned from my husband. If'n you put spots on your skin, you can sometimes fool people inta thinkin' yer sick. If that man…"

55

Grant, understanding dawning, set to work. "But he knows what Hetty looks like."

"In poor light and with bandages we might can fool him," Maude told Grant.

"Let's hope, but what about you?"

"Yer gonna have ta trust me. Suggest ya leave here, just in case," Maude suggested, "an' ya better take the horses."

Grant was torn. He could continue his journey, but what if Hetty should wake up? What if Con returned and found the horses gone? How would Hetty feel about being deserted? He really didn't owe her anything. Still, the questions kept coming one after the other. "And what will you tell Boggs about the horses being gone?"

"Don't ya worry about the horses or that man. As for yer lady, I'll tell her what happened. You get her saddlebags, bring them back here."

With a look at Hetty, Grant went to do as Maude bid.

# CHAPTER
*Fourteen*

**M**aude bathed Hetty's face and hands. *Poor girl is burning up, and somethin' is bothering her,* Maude thought as she did her best to keep Hetty quiet, so she could listen for the doctor or worse, the return of Con Boggs. If what Grant had said was true, there was bound to be trouble.

In her fevered mind, Hetty saw herself writing the names of the books at the school. Kiowa Wells had purchased the books not only for the school, but for the community to use also. Amos Krieder and his new wife Mary Jane had just dropped off the latest group. Hetty was excited, not only for the students, but for the whole community of Kiowa Wells.

"Why am I here, I thought I was on the trail with Grant? Grant, where is Grant?" Hetty cried out. She felt a cool hand on her forehead, heard, "Yer gonna be okay."

Hetty saw herself rubbing her eyes as she lifted her

arms to stretch the kinks from her neck and shoulders. There was a scratch at the door, followed by a groan. The sky continued to darken as she watched the spring storm, the wind whipping the branches of the trees. Drops of rain were trying to fall, attempting to moisten the winter dried ground.

Maude wrung out the cloth she'd placed on Hetty's forehead. She was worried. The fever seemed to be getting worse. *Where was Clover and Doc Brown?* she wondered. Her fear was Hetty would die before they got here.

Meanwhile Hetty looked down at the note in her hand. *No not a note, a letter, a letter for Grant, but where was he?*

Hetty remembered, it had been entrusted to her. Grant's brother Harrison, the injured man, wanted it delivered to Grant. He believed she'd find someone to deliver it. *Maybe, I should find someone, but...* Hetty thought. The wind blew, and the smoke leaked from the stove. Her eyes watered, "darn smoke" she coughed, wiping the tears from her eyes. The school children will be fine, no need to worry about them. School was over and then she laughed. She would only be gone for a few days. *But it was warm, there was no smoke,* Hetty's rational mind said.

Maude heard a horse and buggy outside. Leaving Hetty, she went to the door. Doc Brown was climbing down from his buggy. Walking outside, she looked around. Then, linking her arm with the doctor's she said into his ear, "There's a young woman hit her head. She's runnin' a fever. Plus, a nasty lookin' fellow's out to get her."

Doc Brown placed a hand over Maude's, "I won't give you or her away."

"Thanks, Doc. Told the man she's my sister."

As Doc went into the house, Maude walked up to Clover. "Clover, that woman in there is yer auntie, you 'member that if yer asked."

Clover nodded and set about tending the horses. Who

knew how long Doc Brown would be.

When Doc saw the spots he smiled. It was an old trick, but a good one. He gently removed the bandage from Hetty's head. At the doctor's touch, Hetty moaned, mumbling, "Can't let them know I'm a woman."

Hetty was changing into men's clothes and packing her saddlebags. She took a last look around. then walked to the stable and Odysseus, her gelding, waiting there for her. Three days, six maximum, then she would be back. Started out, the sun to her back, Hetty smiled, "We're off on an adventure, old friend," she informed Odysseus.

"No, no, why am I going backward. I've delivered the message, I'm married," Hetty cried, rolling back and forth.

It took both Maude and the doctor to hold Hetty to the cot. Then Doc gave Hetty a dose of laudanum which helped calm her down.

"Didn't want to do that, but the way she's thrashing around, she's far more likely to hurt herself. In the meantime, we've got to get the fever down," Doc informed Maude.

# CHAPTER
## Fifteen

L ooking over a rock near the cabin, Grant stood watch. He just didn't feel right leaving without making sure Boggs didn't return.

He'd seen the boy come back with the doctor. The man was taking a long time inside, increasing Grant's worry. He was getting ready to find out what was taking so long when Boggs came storming up.

"You lyin'..."

"Sir," Doc Brown ordered as he came to the door. "I have a very sick patient and would appreciate you keeping your voice down."

Boggs was brought up short by the doctor's presence. Then gathering his anger, bellowed, "Well then who's the patient?"

The doctor answered, "It's Maude's sister. She'd been feeling poorly ever since she came. Finally we've diagnosed the measles, and a bad case it is."

Dismounting, Boggs walked towards the door. "Maybe I better see if it's one of the people I'm looking for?"

Grant eased his rifle over the rock, sighting on Boggs, finger pulling back on the trigger as he heard Doc say, "If you must, but if you become ill—" letting his words hang between Boggs and himself.

Boggs slowed his steps. "I'll just peek in the door."

"Be my guest," Doc offered, stepping aside so Boggs could look inside.

Maybe it was Doc's words about getting sick, or something else, but Boggs barely looked in. Returning to his horse, he mounted and rode away.

Grant eased off the trigger, returning to the horses he'd hidden. He felt bad taking Hetty's horse, but leaving it might bring more trouble to Maude. Looking up, Grant said, "I'm not one for praying as you well know, but I sure would appreciate it if you'd keep Hetty safe." Grant mounted up and left the area.

Backtracking, just in case someone was tracking the horses, Grant caught a glimpse of the prison. How he'd hated that place and his time there. If there were any good to come out of that time, it'd toughened him up for the journey ahead. A journey he had to undertake because of his mother. He stuffed down the feelings of betrayal, hate, and revenge. Time enough for that when he'd completed his mission.

Riding north again, Grant thought briefly of the letter that brought Hetty into his life. On reflection, perhaps he should've read it, but that was not possible now. He'd tossed it into the fire.

"Probably just more lies," he mumbled, "and now someone else is suffering because of Mother's lies."

Grant's hold on the reins tightened. He wished he could take his hands and squeeze the life out of his mother. As a substitute he cursed her, his brother and the fates.

"Nothing we can do now but find Swisher and clear my

name," Grant declared, urging the horses into a canter as he resumed the journey into the high country. He just prayed Hetty would heal. He believed she would be better off without him. It wasn't like he'd grown fond of her.

With the two horses, Grant could switch off, making the journey to the Wellington homestead in less time than expected.

The cabin stood on the only level ground for some distance. Pikes Peak lay just to the right, and still had a blanket of snow at the top. He also saw patches of green in this high meadow. The cattle looked like they'd weathered the previous winter well.

Grant had a moment of fear as he rode up to the place. He feared Luke wouldn't talk to him, despite an earlier friendship between the families. Shaking his head, Grant continued forward. He felt it better to just ride in than to sit and worry.

Approaching the cabin, he was greeted by a barking dog. This was followed by a rifle peeking out the window.

"Hello the house," Grant shouted. "Is this the Wellington place?"

"It might be, what you want?" Came a young male voice.

Grant assumed it might be Bob, Luke Wellington's son, but he couldn't be sure. "Looking for Luke Wellington, or at least one of his…"

"Who are you?" Came a demanding voice before Grant had finished.

"Grant, Grant Davis," Grant answered, seeing no reason to lie about who he was.

"That snake, he's in prison," a voice carried back to Grant.

Grant's shoulders started to slump. It seemed his trip had been wasted. Then sitting taller, he called back, "Call me what you want, but I did my time. I'm trying to find Swisher. After I got out, I'd heard you had a place up here."

Grant watched the rifle retreat, and heard a pistol hammer being drawn back from the woodpile to the left.

"Come on in, but be mighty careful," came from the woodpile.

Grant dismounted, and holding the reins in his right hand. He made sure he kept his left away from the pistol on his left thigh. Coming close to the cabin, he tied the horses and walked through the door that opened before him.

The cabin was small, and sparsely furnished. Maybe three people maximum would fit. Grant thought just men were living here now. After seeing the countryside and the tiny cabin, he understood how a woman might like to live elsewhere during the winter.

To the right of the door stood a young man about fifteen. Behind him, Grant could feel the pistol pushing him farther inside. He might have been able to turn and disarm the man, but he came on a peaceful mission. He assumed the person behind him was the one by the woodpile.

"I presume that's you behind me, Luke?"

"Could be. Step on in, let's take a look at you."

Grant did as the man asked, all the while feeling uneasy.

"Let me have that gun," the man ordered.

Again Grant complied, only to have his pistol returned after just a few seconds. He pondered keeping the gun out, but the next words decided for him and he returned it to its place on his thigh.

"Wanted to make sure it was you, you looking some different," Luke said. "Turn around, let me take a look at you."

Grant was perplexed, but relieved he hadn't been hit over the head or shot. "Why all the precautions?"

Luke indicated the chairs by the table. "There's those riding through here what's trouble. But tell me why you're riding this high up?"

# CHAPTER
*Sixteen*

T he next day, Maude greeted Doc Brown at the door. "Doc," Maude said as they walked in, "she's still got a fever, and she ain't movin'."

Entering the sick area, Doc checked the injury to Hetty's head. "Her head wound is clean and should heal. Might have a scar, but that won't matter none if we can't get the fever down."

"What could it be?" Maude wondered. "She just all of a sudden got quiet and hasn't moved much since."

The doctor shook his head. Placing a hand on Hetty's cheek, and checking her pulse, eyebrows drawn together. Shaking his head, he told Maude, "Maude, let's get her out of these clothes so I can check her more thoroughly."

"But," Maude began.

"This is no time for modesty," Doc Brown barked.

Maude immediately set about helping the doctor remove the rest of Hetty's clothing, including the binding she'd been wearing.

Once the clothes were removed, Doc Brown covered Hetty with blanket, only exposing her shoulders and arms. Maude stood by as the doctor began checking the exposed areas.

"What you doin', Doc?"

"There has to be something else we've been missing, that bump on the head shouldn't have caused a fever to last this long."

Once the doctor examined the exposed area he lowered the sheet to examine Hetty's torso and back. It was on her back he found a large, red, raised area that appeared to be filled with puss. Turning to his bag, Doc Brown pulled out a sharp blade. He made an incision across the raised area. Looking up at Maude he directed, "We need to clean this well. Do you have some clean rags and soap?"

Maude nodded and moved to the kitchen area. Pouring hot water from a teakettle into a bowl, Maude grabbed up the soap and returned to Hetty's cot. The doctor draped the sheet across Hetty's shoulders, torso and legs, leaving the incision exposed. While Maude cleaned the wound, he continued checking. Farther down he located yet another area on Hetty's right leg. He repeated the lancing procedure, with Maude cleaning that area also.

Upon completing his examination, and finding no other wounds, they left Hetty on her side, now covered again with blankets.

"You'll need to continue trying to get the fever down and make sure that you keep the areas we lanced uncovered and clean. May be she was reacting to whatever caused those red marks. My guess is it was an insect like a spider caused the infection."

"Hope yer right." Maude said. "But she didn't react, 'cept a couple of moans, while we worked on 'er."

Doc rinsed his instruments in the hot water and put things back into his bag. He looked again at Hetty, feeling her cheek, and checking her heartbeat. "Her heart sounds strong and she's young. There is hope for a complete recovery."

"I'll say prayers," Maude told Doc as the two walked out to his buggy.

"You take good care of that sister of yours, I'll be back out in a couple of days. If there's any major change just send Clover in for me." Doc said in a loud voice.

Maude gave Doc Brown an odd look, but said, "Thanks Doc, appreciate it."

With a nod and a wave, Doc turned the buggy and headed back to town. Maude returned to the cabin and Hetty. She stood looking at Hetty lying there so quiet, her face pale, but it seemed to Maude perhaps she was breathing a bit easier.

Standing there, Maude remembered Doc's words about hope, then it hit her what he'd said as he left. There might still be someone watching the cabin. She and Clover were going to have to be extra careful. It would not do to have gone to all this trouble to keep Hetty safe, only to say one wrong thing and put her in danger again.

# CHAPTER
## Seventeen

"I'm looking for folks who could clear my name," Grant told Luke, "It's bad enough I spent time in prison but…"

"Never did believe it, but the evidence," Luke interrupted. "But that's past, might be wise to just move, change your name."

"Maybe, but I don't want to, and with a—" Grant let the sentence hang. It had meant so much to him to clear his name, get his life back, while serving his sentence. It had been the reason he put up with the other prisoners' talk, and some of the guards' meanness. Keeping to himself and out of trouble was why he'd been released early. What Luke said might be a good idea, but he just couldn't let it go.

"Believe it or not son, think I understand."

"Thanks. Could use some understanding." Grant thought Hetty understood, but she wasn't here. Instead she was lying ill in a strangers home. Well, Maude seemed like a good sort of person. Now maybe Luke was going to help. "Like I said, I'm looking for Swisher," Grant finished.

"Grant, he's the one who testified," Luke reminded him, concern in his voice. "You sure he would help you?"

"He might not want to, but I gotta persuade him," Grant stated. "I know right after, he'd a fair amount of money in his pocket." The old anger against the man, and his lost years slammed against the wall he'd set up in his mind.

"Always wondered about that. Gave his notice a couple of weeks after you were sent up."

"You're probably the only one who believes me," anger and hurt creeping into his voice as Grant stared out the window.

"Boy, I'm not one to give advice, but revenge and long-held anger won't get you anywhere. Move on, find yourself a good woman and get on with your life."

Grant looked over to Luke. He'd always been kind to him, especially after his father's death. Grabbing the table's edge, Grant gripped so hard his knuckles turned white. As he felt the rough wood under his fingers, his knuckles relaxed, returning to their natural color. "I have a wife," Grant said in a soft voice.

"A wife!" Luke exclaimed. "Congratulations boy. How and when did this happen?"

"Recently," Grant answered, returning his eyes to the world outside the window. He had reservations about saying more. It wasn't that he felt Luke would say anything, but Boggs had a way of getting answers. On the heel of that thought was worry for Luke's safety if Boggs trailed him here.

Seeing the worry on Grant's face, Luke asked "What's bothering you?"

The silence stretched as Grant continued staring out the window. He wondered if Hetty would recover. Part of him was angry at her. He was even more angry at himself, but he didn't want to admit the reason why. He wondered if Boggs had left Maude and Hetty alone. He also wondered if Boggs was on his way here to make him pay for escaping. But why would he want to make him pay, why be so upset by being thwarted by him and Hetty. Nothing made sense. Grant shook his head in frustration. Turning, he looked at Luke. "The less you know…"

"Grant, let me be the judge," Luke interrupted. "We all make our own choices. If there's something going to happen here, then the more I know, the better prepared I can be."

Grant sat still, then relaxing his shoulders, he began talking.

# CHAPTER
### *Eighteen*

**M**aude met Doc Brown at the door the following afternoon when he came to check on Hetty. "Good news Doc, fever seems to 'ave broke last night and sister's been sleeping peacefully ever since."

Doc smiled, the tired lines on his face easing somewhat. "That's mighty good news. I'd have been here earlier, but some dang fool kid was swinging in a tree, fell and broke his arm."

"Well, ya know, kids'll be kids," Maude laughed as the two walked inside. Once away from the door, Maude added, "Seems you were correct about somethin' causin' the fever. Whatever it was you lanced musta been poisonin' the poor girl."

"Well it was touch and go, now we just gotta keep those areas clean, and try to get some food into her."

With a grin, Maude looked back over her shoulder, saying, "Now Doc this ain't no girl, she's a young woman, a rather striking one at that."

Doc Brown just grinned, following Maude into the sick area. "At my age Maudie, even you are a young girl."

Maude blushed, gently hitting Doc on the shoulder.

Doc moved over to Hetty, pulling the sheet aside. He lifted the gown covering Hetty when she opened her eyes, fear and anger sparking as she rose up to shove the doctor away.

Maude came over, gently taking Hetty's hand saying, "Hetty, my name is Maude. You've been unconscious and runnin' a fever fer the last three days. Doc Brown here's been comin' to see you every day. He found where somethin' bit you. He's just checking to make sure that yer healin' correctly."

Hetty looked from Maude to the doctor and back again. Then her eyes took in the cabin, the cot where she lay, the gown that covered her. She blushed when she realized the bindings she'd been wearing were no longer wrapped around her torso. In a weak voice she asked, "Where's Grant?"

Maude looked toward the doctor, and the two exchanged a look. Hetty caught that look and immediately became fearful. She asked again, trying to rise from the cot, "Where's Grant?"

"I'll tell ya the whole story after Doc Brown here finishes what he's got to do. I promise I'll tell ya everythin', but we need to let the good doctor get back to his patients."

Hetty again looked at the old man, his brown eyes both kind and sympathetic. "I know this is unusual, but you've been through a tough time young lady, not only from the cut on your head but from whatever bit you causing you to pass out and run a fever."

With a slight nod, Hetty lay back on the cot, closing her eyes while the doctor examined the two bites he'd lanced earlier. He was so gentle and quick, Hetty almost hadn't realized what he was doing except for where the air hit the exposed areas.

"Well young lady, if you'll take it easy, and do as I and Maudie say, I think you're going to make a full recovery." Then turning to Maude he added, "At this point I don't see any reason for me coming back until next Monday."

Hetty nodded, saying, "Thank you sir, I appreciate all you have done."

The doctor patted her hand and after a quick examination of Hetty's head walked with Maude to the door, giving her instructions. He waved and headed back to town.

Just before leaving, he whispered to Maude, "Take care, try not to let her get upset. She doesn't know what went on, and I leave it to you to break it to her gently."

Maude gave Doc a smile, "I'll do my best. Poor thing, but she may surprise us. Think she's stronger than we realize."

Maude waited until the Doctor was out of sight, then taking a deep breath, headed back inside. She found Clover sitting next to Hetty's cot, telling her about their new milk cow and the cream and butter they sold in town.

Maude started to say something, but Hetty gave a slight shake of her head, then turned her attention back to Clover.

"Thank you for telling me Clover, do you milk the cow?"

Clover nodded yes, then proceeded to tell Hetty about the chickens and the eggs they laid and how he'd named each and every one. "Think my favorite is Bessie, she's always following me 'round."

Maude put her arm around her son's shoulders, "Why don't ya go out 'n check for eggs. It's 'bout time to milk the cow, too."

With a smile at Hetty, Clover went to do as his mother bid.

"You have a fine son, Maude."

"Hope he weren't botherin' ya too much," Maude said

as she began straightening up the room. "Misses his father, but understands he'll return someday."

Hetty noticed how Maude's shoulders slumped and averted her eyes when speaking of her husband. "Would I be prying if I asked…"

Maude kept her back to Hetty. Hetty feared she'd overstepped her bounds when Maude sighed. "He's in prison. Yer husband knew 'bout it, but you was unconscious when we talked. They sentenced him fer shootin' a man what was botherin' me."

"Maude, if there's one thing I know it's that no man has the right to bother a woman regardless of what they say." That Maude was exposed to more than just bothering made Hetty angry at the unfairness of life. Not only was Maude's husband being punished, but his wife and son were suffering also.

"But," Maude paused, then looking at Hetty. "Ya might be right, but them jurors blamed my Jack fer protectin' me. Said I wasn't a good woman, but I am."

Hetty didn't know what to say, but she wanted to help ease the pain. Maude had taken her in, cared for her, while still taking care of her home and her son. That wasn't the actions of a 'bad woman'. Hetty wasn't sure, but somehow she would help Maude and Clover, and Jack.

"But 'nough 'bout me," Maude said, "Doc Brown says yer ta take it easy. Long's we keep yer fever down an' them bites clean, ya should get well pretty fast."

Hetty took the hint, letting the subject of Maude's husband Jack drop. "Well, I confess I'm feeling a little tired, but," here Hetty hesitated. She didn't see Grant anywhere, and since neither Maude nor Clover mentioned anything about him, she knew he probably wasn't here. But where was he? Still she needed to know.

"Maude, where's Grant?"

Maude sat on the edge of the cot taking one of Hetty's hands in hers. "A man named Boggs came, and yer husband said we was ta protect ya, not let him find ya. Said he was headin' out ta take care o' the errand he was on when ya got sick. Said fer ya ta head on back home when ya was feelin' better."

"And the horses?" Hetty felt she knew the answer but wanted Maude to verify it.

"He took 'em with him so's Boggs wouldn't know you's here. But he left yer things, they's under the bed."

Hetty wanted to cry. Maude might think it was something she did, and Hetty didn't want to put any additional burden on the woman. Taking a deep breath, she said, "Thank you for telling me. I was afraid something had happened to my horse, Odysseus. If Grant has him, everything should be okay." Even as she said it, Hetty prayed she was correct.

"Course everythin' will be okay," Maude said, patting Hetty's hand. "That man loves ya somethin' fierce."

Maude's words shocked Hetty. Nothing that Grant had done gave any indication of any true feelings for her. Hetty knew he was a good man. He'd made up the story about her being his lost wife when he could have left her to Boggs and his men. He even went through with the marriage ceremony. Thinking the part of the vows about honoring and cherishing, Hetty felt her cheeks grow warm. Looking away, so Maude wouldn't see the tears her eyes, Hetty plucked at her cover.

"He's been all that is kind," Hetty whispered.

Maude looked at Hetty. "Ya jest rest Mrs. Davis, everythin' will turn out fine."

"I pray you're right."

Maude smiled at Hetty, then turned and went into the kitchen area and began preparing the next meal.

Hetty lay back, closing her eyes against the pain and fear she had for the future. The more she tried to relax, the more uneasy she became. *What's going to happen to me? What might happen to Grant? How about Odysseus?* Over and over the thoughts, the questions, kept running through her mind, flashing pictures behind her eyelids.

*Enough!* Hetty admonished herself. There was nothing she could do about any of the things she was worried about. Instead, Hetty turned to the things that she could do, like how could she help Maude and Clover? What could she do to help clear Grant's name? Was there anything she could do for Maude's husband? A sense of peace came over Hetty. She fell into a restful sleep thinking about what she could do for those who had done so much for her.

# CHAPTER
*Nineteen*

G rant took off farther into the mountains and the mining district Luke thought Swisher may have headed for. He thought it would take about two days riding along the back trails, just in case he was followed.

Those two days brought uncomfortable questions. "Why did I bring her along after we got away from Boggs?" Grant asked the horses. It was true Hetty would have been safer if he'd sent her back. "Why didn't she leave?"

Laughing, Grant thought how silly he would sound if anyone heard him. At the same time, why was he keeping her horse? Was he hoping he could go back to her after he cleared his name? Would Hetty be glad when he personally returned her horse? Would she welcome him?

When he lay down at night, Grant's thoughts were on Hetty and her recovery.

76

Grant was even more exhausted than when he'd laid down at night when he awakened. He'd stare at his fire, down to a few dim coals, and think of Hetty. "Stop it," Grant said, that second morning, "she will be fine."

Grant wondered if anyone would notice if he just let it all go, gave up and ran away. He was tired, cold and just didn't care. He felt like the lone stick in the Aesop's fable he'd heard as a child. Not strong enough to make it on his own.

In the midst of these thoughts floated the faces of his father, his brother. Then Hetty's face appeared, her eyes sparking with anger, then her pale face as he remembered when she lay on the ground.

"Okay, you win," Grant said as he rose and gently blew on the coals to build the fire up again. Heating the coffee left from last night, Grant set about getting ready for the trip to Virginia City to continue his hunt for Swisher.

After saddling up, Grant turned in the direction where he'd left Hetty. "Thank you. Here's hoping you are recovering," Grant said, then as he mounted up, "wish me luck, wife."

Just before noon, Grant rode over the mountain and into the Tin Cup mining district. Grant wondered what he'd find, if the stories about the wide open wildness of the town were true.

Giving Nelly the go-ahead, he and the horses started down the mountain. He glanced back at Odysseus. If the town were as wild as they said, he should've left Hetty's horse with Luke. Odysseus was a fine looking animal, one a person would steal without thinking twice.

Still, Grant found he couldn't part with the gelding. Pulling over into a stand of trees, Grant switched saddles to Odysseus for the ride into town. "I know you're not used to other riders, but this way I can help keep you safe," he told the horse. Odysseus gave a shake and a nod as if he understood.

Even for the noon hour, the town appeared rather

boisterous. Grant could hear the roar from where he stood about a half a mile away on the mountainside. "You'd think such a new town would be a bit quieter," he said as he prepared to mount up.

"You might at that mister," came a voice off to Grant's right. "Most folks come in from one of the trails."

Grant stiffened. He cursed himself for not being more vigilant instead of thinking about his wife. But then his wife wasn't like any other woman he'd ever met. "There's a trail from the East?" Grant asked to cover himself. That he was aware of such a trail was true, but he'd hope to get into Virginia City, then out with little notice.

"Mister, there's trails from the east, west, and south. Gettin' so a person can't move through these here mountains without running into some fools looking to get rich quick. You one o' them?"

"No," Grant assured the voice. "Heard of Virginia City and wondered if it was anything like the ones in Nevada and Montana? Plus, it would be the kind of town a man I grew up around would gravitate to."

"He one of them pretend prospectors, or o' them that prey on the fools?"

Grant wondered if he should trust this voice, or lie. He assumed the person to be an old timer to the area, but when the rush for riches was on, you couldn't tell. Hedging, Grant replied, "Couldn't tell, haven't seen him for some time, but things came up, back where I'm from that I needed to talk to him about."

"If'n' you think it's worth it to head into that den o' thieves, take my advice—don't."

Since the voice hadn't made any threats, or tried to shoot him, Grant turned toward the voice saying, "I'd prefer not to, but don't have much choice. Perhaps, if you're inclined, you could tell me what to watch out for. Maybe that way I could get in, see if the man's there and get out."

"Why should I do that? You might be lyin' just to…,"

the voice stopped.

Grant had the idea, from the way the conversation was going, he might have stumbled onto a secret claim. Perhaps he should make a break, ride away. Yet, if this person could tell him more about the area, about the town, it might be quicker and safer.

"Tell you what, how 'bout I give you my gun, and we just sit here. No need to go anywhere else." Grant wrapped the reins of the horses around a nearby bush, before continuing. "To tell the truth, if I didn't need to try to find this guy Swisher, I'd not have even come this way."

Grant took a chance and sitting on a rock, continued with a smile, "I'd be with my new wife." Even as he said it, a part of Grant did want to be with Hetty, but until he cleared his name... *No*, he thought, *I would never be good enough for her.*

"You can keep your gun, follow me."

Grant untied the horses and followed. They walked over a hidden trail through the brush and pines. Grant remained alert, hand near his pistol. As they broke into a clearing, a chuckle carried back to him. His guide turned around and Grant came face-to-face with a little gnome, about four and a half feet tall, lighting up a pipe. The smoke rose to form a wreath around a black-hatted face. The closer he looked, the more sure Grant became that the person might be a woman.

"Pull your eyes back inta your head. Ain't you never heard of a woman prospector?"

"I'd heard, but never met one," Grant answered, his cheeks heating as he looked away.

"It's all right, used to it. Folks in town just sort of make fun a 'Crazy Molly', leastwise that's what they call me. Think I'm crazy. Leave me alone, which suits me just fine."

"Aren't you afraid they might try to hurt you? Or jump your claim?"

"Nah, never taken too much color into town at any one time. Safer that way."

Grant looked more closely at the woman. She didn't seem to be as old as he thought. "I hope you're correct. If the town is as wild as you say…"

Molly interrupted, "That's right thoughtful o' you, but there's other places that's easy to get to."

"Well, if you'd like, I can enter the town from another direction, keep your location secret," Grant offered.

"Be right thoughtful."

"Consider it done. But you said you could tell me something about the town."

"So's I did. How about some tea while we talk?" Molly said as she moved into the cabin, motioning Grant to enter as she did.

As much as Grant wanted to find Swisher and finish his quest, he felt Molly might be lonely. A little more time wouldn't make that much difference. There was also the chance Molly's knowledge of the town and the area would save him time. The more he knew before entering Virginia City, the better off he thought he would be.

Setting a cup of tea in front of Grant, Molly said, "If you enter 'bout dark, might be safer, 'specially with them horses."

Grant nodded in agreement. "You may be right. When I started out to find Swisher, it seemed best to have two horses. I could switch off, cutting the journey, and get in and out of places quicker." Grinning, he added, "Just in case someone should take offense at my questions."

"Smart, real smart, 'specially in this area."

Preferring coffee, Grant didn't want to hurt Molly's feelings, he took a sip. "You said you could tell me something about the town."

# CHAPTER
*Twenty*

A week after the accident, Hetty was bored. She was still weak. Her sickbed was feeling like a prison and she wanted to get up, get moving. The doctor had been by and when he left, Hetty saw him talking to Maude. If she could get moving, perhaps she could find Grant. She understood why he left, but she was still hurt by his desertion.

"Hetty," Maude broke into Hetty's thoughts. "Doc Brown said if ya was up ta it, and took it easy, ya could move ta a chair."

*Finally a small bit of variety* Hetty thought, "I would like that." Then thinking of Boggs and his men, she asked, "Has a man, Convover Boggs come by?"

"He come by, but that man o' yours'd left. He told us 'bout Boggs, so when he come, we convinced 'im ya was my sister. Since then, we's not ever seen him come back. 'Spect he bought ya bein' my sister."

Maude didn't want to worry Hetty with Doc Brown's suspicions. She and Clover hadn't noticed anyone around, but they were still keeping an eye out. What bothered Maude was why Boggs was so intent on getting Hetty and Grant. Seemed mighty mean. Maude wondered if her husband had to deal with men like that in prison. The thought sent a chill up her spine.

"I hope you are right, I wouldn't want anything to happen to any of you on my account," Hetty told Maude. She hoped Maude was right, but knowing Boggs, she wasn't so sure. He was probably trailing Grant out of anger at his taking her away. But something told her he probably had someone watching the place. She'd seen movement outside the window, although she could have imagined it in her fever. One thing she knew, she would need to be careful when she left here.

Maude called Clover and the two helped Hetty from her sickbed to a chair near the door. Hetty was thankful for all the two had done while she'd been so sick.

"Thank you," Hetty gasped out. The short walk, even with help, took more energy than she'd believed. She sank into the chair, and breathlessly continued. "Guess I'm weaker than I thought."

Maude tucked a blanket around Hetty, while Clover went back outside to check on their horse and chop more wood.

"You was mighty sick there fer awhile. We was worried, but Doc Brown, he's a pretty good doctor."

"I have so much to thank all of you for. Maybe I can repay your kindness someday," Hetty said, thinking of the ideas she'd been working on while recovering.

Hetty hoped Grant was taking good care of Odysseus. A part of her was angry he'd taken him, but she now understood. Boggs knew her horse and it would've brought trouble to the very people who were caring for her. She was thankful Grant had been so thoughtful. Still, there was a painful hole in her heart when she thought of not seeing the gelding again.

"Ya missin' yer man?" Maude asked as she finished tucking the blanket around Hetty.

"Yes." It seemed easier to just agree. Maude didn't need to know it was her horse she was thinking about. As for Grant, well at some point he was going to have to forgive those who hurt him, if he didn't get killed first. Following that thought, Hetty wondered if she would be able to forgive Grant for leaving. *Who was she kidding?* she thought. *Grant didn't owe her anything, it was she who owed him for saving her life, more than once.*

She frowned, Grant refused to leave her thoughts. She prayed he'd find what he was searching for, but she knew he'd moved on. He'd helped her to safety, his job with her was over.

While thinking of Grant, feeling the sun on her skin, she decided to put the plan she'd conceived into action. "Maude, you have any paper and a pencil?" Hetty asked. If all worked out, the plan would not only take care of her, but possibly Grant and Maude's family also.

"Yes," Maude replied as she went to get the requested items. "Ya want ta write yer husband?"

"Well, it's more writing to help him."

Maude dug through a chest and brought Hetty the paper. First, Hetty would let Josie know she was okay and to be expecting a package within a week or so. She also asked Josie if her husband Will would investigate the Davis family and their history. Something Grant said had been bothering her and she hoped Will could find out more about Grant's mother, and his father's death.

Finishing up, Hetty felt tired, but more at ease about the future. She might never see Grant again but she'd done what she could.

"Maude, isn't Doc Brown due back soon?"

"Spectin' ta see him tomorrow," Maude answered. "Ya startin' ta feel poorly again?"

With a slight shake of her head, Hetty answered, "I'm

feeling better. I think getting some fresh air and sunshine helped." Hetty rose slowly and made her way back to the cot unaided.

"See," she said as she lay back, a tired sigh escaping. "As for Doc, I was hoping he might mail a letter to my friend. I know she's worried, and this way if someone's watching, they hopefully won't suspect anything."

"Ya might be right," Maude agreed. Then Maude looked embarrassed, but squaring her shoulders, she asked, "Could ya write a letter to my husband?"

"Of course," Hetty replied.

"Thank ya. I never learned readin' an' writin', but my husband, he knows."

"Do you want to do it now?"

"Yer tired. Maybe later, after I've a chance to think on what I want ta say."

"Just let me know."

Hetty lay back, satisfied she had taken back some control over her future. Maude's request gave Hetty the beginning of an idea of how to help Maude and her son. Then she thought of Odysseus. Hetty rose up on her elbow, "Maude, if I'm gone and Grant should return, tell him I've returned to our home."

"Ya sure ya don't want ta wait?"

"I think I would feel better getting you out of danger," Hetty replied. "But I'm not leaving that soon," she finished with a laugh. But in her mind, Hetty knew it wouldn't be much longer. There were things that needed to be done, and she could only do so much with letters. She'd be making her own trip, and soon.

A part of her really did want to be going now, but she knew she was too weak to do any major traveling. Maude and Clover, along with Doc Brown had been so kind. Still, as long as Boggs was out there, knowing she was still alive, no one would be safe.

Thoughts of Boggs made Hetty think. She would take precautions as she traveled back to Kiowa Wells. She missed her students, even though it was summer. As a married woman, would she still be able to teach? Without Grant around, she would have to make a living somehow, but how she didn't know. Somehow she would make out, but in her heart, she wished she could have a future with Grant. At the same time, as kind as he'd been, he didn't need to be saddled with an ugly, spinster wife.

"Mrs. Davis," Maude said, interrupting Hetty's thoughts, "Ya don't worry 'bout us, it's you needs ta take care. That husband o' yers would be mighty upset if'n we let anythin' happen ta ya.."

"I know," Hetty responded, fighting the tears of despair at the untruth of Maude's words. "But he would also not want you hurt. When I'm strong enough, I have things I need to do to help him." *At least that was true*, Hetty thought.

"Ya two remind me how much my man an' I luv each other. It's why I come here, ta be close, even if'n I don't go visit."

Hetty rose and gave the woman a hug. "I know you will be together soon and make a great life for yourself and your son."

Maude wiped her eyes. "Bless ya and yer husband. Now, it's time ya get some more rest."

Hetty let Maude help her get settled, but just as she closed her eyes, she saw movement outside the window up in the rocks.

# CHAPTER
## Twenty-One

G rant arrived in town as the light faded behind the mountains. True to his word to Molly, he'd ridden around the town and entered from the west.

"You needn't worry about the marshal," Molly had said. "Seems like he's made arrangements to not interfere with what's going on." She laughed. "He just pretends ta roust a few drunks over to the jail, then lets 'em go afore ever gettin' them inside."

Riding by the lights of various businesses and saloons, Grant could believe what Molly had said. In front of one of the saloons, two men burst through the door.

Pulling the horses off to one side, he watched as the two men circled and wove around each other. One had a shoe in his hand, the other a coat.

"I'll make you take back your words," the man with the shoe shouted. He swung on the other man, who used the coat like a rope, capturing the attackers arm, pulling the man forward. When the two were close enough, they set about trying to beat each other senseless.

When it looked like the two would kill each other, out walked a man who raised his pistol and fired toward the two men.

Time slowed down, the street quieted. Grant cast his gaze from the elegantly dressed man with the gun to the two combatants. Neither appeared harmed by the shot. That he hadn't killed or wounded one of them was a miracle. The two men glared at each other, yet stood quiet as the man spoke.

"Conner, return Sam's shoe to him. Hunter, the coat—," the man ordered, his voice soft, yet menacing.

Cowed by the man, the two meekly did as they were told. "You will both have your wages docked for the next two weeks to pay for the damages."

Grant caught a flare of anger in Hunter's eyes, for both the man with the gun and Conner. It was just a brief look, but it gave Grant the feeling he was watching a mouse wanting to attack a snake, but knowing it was death to do so.

Evidently, this man wielded so much power that people submitted to his will. Grant shrugged his shoulders, it wasn't his concern. He just needed to find out if Swisher was here, and if so where he could find him.

Riding on to the stable, Grant put his two horses up himself when no one answered his call.

"Mighty nice horse flesh," a man said from behind Grant. "Be here long?"

Grant glanced back at the man, "Maybe. You own this place?"

"Yep, and two bits per horse, or two dollars a week," the hostler said. Looking Grant over, he added, "Payable in advance."

Grant pulled out the money for one night. "Looking for an acquaintance so it'll depend on whether I can find him or not."

"Mayhap I might know him," the man offered, as he reached over to pat Odysseus, only to have the gelding try to bite him.

"Mighty skittish, ain't he," the man offered as he jumped back.

"Kind of a one person horse, but both of them suit me just fine," Grant said.

The man nodded, rubbing his hand, "About that friend?"

"Man named Swisher."

"Seems familiar, but not sure why?" the hostler replied. "You know, you might check at the Monument saloon. Run by a man named Warner. It's up the street about a block."

"Is it a well-dressed, dark-haired man?" Grant asked.

"Yep, that's him. Might say he kinda runs the town, him and Mrs. Smith."

"Mrs. Smith?"

The hostler looked uncomfortable, "Well, she owns the hotel here an' a couple other places in other towns. Warner, he don't mess with her."

Grant digested the information the hostler offered, wondering about the dynamics between the two powers in town. "Thanks, I'll be back shortly."

The man smiled, putting the money in his pocket. "Luck."

"Thanks." Grant turned, walking back to where the fight had taken place. He stood across the street, staring toward the saloon. He wasn't sure why he hesitated, but something was holding him back. He never wavered before, but the hair on the back of his neck was standing on end.

The young man walked by, and Grant thought of Hetty, how she dressed as a boy to try to find him. He saw how that turned out. "Well, wife, here goes," he said as he prepared for what he didn't know. He walked across the street and through the saloon doors. He hoped to find Swisher quickly, get him to write down the truth. If he died here—that could be a possibility—he wanted to make sure Hetty wouldn't be saddled with a husband who carried the label of outlaw.

Grant watched as Warner and a young cowhand were arguing at the end of the bar. He also noticed a girl, dressed in blue, gaudy jewelry around wrist and neck. She was peeping through a back door, intent on the young man.

"But, I love her. I intend to marry Constance," the young man insisted.

Warner waved hand, and a bouncer took hold of the young man. "Constance will remain here until I say she can go," Warner said.

As he was thrust through the door, he called back, "You'll see, love overcomes everything."

Grant saw the girl put hand to mouth, as tears slid down her cheeks. The sight brought bile to Grant's throat, his fist clenched. Breathing deep, telling himself it was none of his affair, Grant approached Warner.

"Pardon," Grant smiled, "are you Mr. Warner? The hostler said you might know the whereabouts of an acquaintance of mine named Swisher."

Warner looked over at Grant, "I am, and how do you know Swisher?" Warner asked, as he took in Grant's dusty appearance.

"Grew up around the same area. Heard he might be here, thought we might catch up on old times."

Warner stared at Grant, as if looking at an insect. "He was here, but he moved on to Leadville."

"Well, it was worth a try since I was in the area," Grant said. "Thanks."

With a cold smile Warner offered, "Have a drink?"

Grant wanted out of the place, but felt one drink he could manage without getting into trouble. It wouldn't hurt to stay on the good side of Warner, and he might learn a bit more about Swisher.

# CHAPTER
*Twenty - Two*

H etty was feeling better, able to eat, and walk short distances without help.

"Need ta get more meat on yer bones," Maude told Hetty as they returned from picking flowers.

Hetty grinned, "And I suppose you have some special recipe that will do the trick?"

Hetty watched as Maude blushed. A mutual respect and affection had developed between them. For her part, Hetty could tell Maude was someone who had so much to share with the world, and blossomed when able to do just that.

"I was thinkin' some beans an' corn pone would be a mighty good way ta start."

Hetty had let slip how much she loved that combination as a child, so Maude made it for her. Of course, eating it three days in a row was a bit much. However, Hetty would rather cut out her tongue then hurt Maude. That affection was making it difficult for Hetty to tell Maude she needed to leave.

It was during the evening meal that Hetty broached the subject. Doc Brown had come by and given Hetty a clean bill of health. He'd remained for the meal.

"Doc Brown, might I bother you for some suggestions for getting into town?"

Before Doc could answer, Maude cut in, "Clover kin take ya. Not that yer not welcome ta stay long as ya'd like."

Hetty turned questioning eyes to the woman. Seeing the look, Maude added, "Know ya want ta find that husband of yers."

Tears slipped from the corners of Hetty's eyes.

Misunderstanding, Maude smiled, "Hetty, ya's always welcome here, but ya got a life ta live an' ya can't do it here."

Words caught in Hetty's throat. Both Doc and Clover squirmed, not sure of what they should do.

Rising, Hetty went to the older woman, hugging her tightly. "You've done more for me than you know. I only hope I can do as much for you."

"Ya already helped. Now I know my man is doing okay and..." Maude stopped as tears sprang to her eyes. "Now look at us, think we could use a change? What about..."

"Think that's good advice," Clover burst out.

The adults laughed. "Well," Doc said, "it's time I got back, you stop by when you get back to town."

With the goodbyes done, Maude turned to Hetty, "I've a dress I kin take in ta fit ya."

"Maude, I have clothes."

"Hetty, them's men's clothes. If'n yer in a dress ya might fool the folks who's followin' ya."

Hetty didn't think it would work, but Maude wouldn't be turned away from giving Hetty the dress. Hetty realized to do anything more to change Maude's mind would only be an insult.

Two days later, the dress was fitted and Hetty prepared to take her leave. Clover had hitched the horse to the wagon, and stored her packed saddle bags under the seat.

Hetty approached Maude, "Would you mind fastening this locket? My fingers are still a bit clumsy."

Maude took the locket, taking in the delicate etchings, and the patina of age. "It's mighty purty."

"My grandmother gave it to me," Hetty smiled, turning her back to Maude. Maude fastened the chain, the locket falling down across the lace around the dress's neck.

"We're lucky, even if'n the world don't think so," Maude said, moving around to face Hetty. "We's both got husbands what care fer us."

Despite Hetty's disbelief in Maude's insistence that Grant cared for her, Hetty wouldn't hurt Maude's feelings by arguing with her.

"An' I thought it might be nice if'n I rode inta town with ya," Maude added. "Ain't ben ta town since..."

"Of course," Hetty's laughter interrupted Maude's speech. "I'd enjoy the company, plus, I don't know the town at all."

Clover climbed into the seat, but Maude and Hetty sat in the back, legs dangling like a couple of schoolgirls. If anyone had come by, the laughter would've reinforced that idea.

Slowly they made their way, both women laughing, talking, and keeping an eye out for anyone following. Not for one minute did Hetty think the dress would fool anyone.

"I'd like to check the train schedule when we get into town," Hetty said. "Without Odysseus, train travel would probably be the safest way to head back to Kiowa Wells."

"Station's near the edge o' town," Clover added from the front seat.

"You know you can visit me any time," Hetty offered to Maude and Clover.

Maude gave Hetty a sad smile. Hetty knew Maude didn't think she'd be welcomed, but Hetty knew everyone would love the woman. Before Maude could reply, Hetty saw a new three-story brick building going up.

"What's that?" Hetty asked.

A passerby hearing the question, shouting the answer, pride in his voice, "That's the new school, and we have a military academy being built also."

"It looks beautiful," Hetty called back, "you have a right to be proud." Looking over at Maude, Hetty caught a look of want and sadness. It gave her an idea.

"Maude, is there a bank?"

"O' course, why da ya ask?" Maude responded.

Hetty didn't want to make Maude uncomfortable or hurt her feelings, but she still wanted to do something to repay Maude's kindness. At Maude's questioning look, Hetty said, "I want to withdraw some funds to pay for my passage back home and," she paused, then went on, "and I'd like to give you a gift."

"Ain't no need," Maude protested.

"I know, but seeing the school gave me an idea," Hetty started. As Maude started to protest, Hetty interrupted "Maude, please hear me out." Maude quieted, but Hetty could see she was uncomfortable.

"Maude, you have been a dear friend, I want to stay in touch. Please, I would like to pay for a tutor so that we can write each other."

Maude remained quiet so long that Hetty was fearful she'd hurt Maude's feelings beyond repair. She glanced over at the older woman, catching a tear traversing Maude's cheek.

"Maude, I'm sorry, I just wanted—"

Maude grabbed Hetty's hands, "I'd like that. but…," Maude stopped, looking at Hetty. Then she added in a rush, "Da ya have the money? What'll yer husband say?"

Hetty smiled, reaching over to hug Maude. "Maude, my Grandmam made sure I would be fine, no matter what."

Maude's eyes grew wide as Hetty added, "May I do this for you?"

Before Maude could answer, people began ranting,

running toward the river. Clover pulled the cart over to get out of the way. As people went by words like, "tragic", accident", "who found the body," reached their ears.

# CHAPTER
## Twenty-Three

T he two women exchanged a look as Maude commented, "Makes ya wonder, so near da prison."

"Surely there's been no escapes?" Hetty replied.

"Ain't been one I heard of," Maude said. "Might be Doc Brown…"

Before Maude could finish, Doc Brown came rushing by. Seeing Hetty and Maude, he paused in his rush, "If you came in to see me, it may be a bit before I'll get to you. Seems the body of a girl has been found in the river. They just dragged her to shore," at Maude's questioning look he added, "Yes, she's dead. They're saying her death was rather brutal. Now I must go," he added as he hurried away.

"Wonder who?" Maude said, then seeing Hetty's pale face, turned toward Clover. "Clover, think ya should head over ta the bank."

"Thank you," Hetty said, her voice barely above a whisper.

Maude turned back toward Hetty, to see the younger woman shaking, her eyes haunted.

"What's wrong?"

If Hetty heard the question, she gave no indication. Maude reached over to pull Hetty into an embrace. Hetty pulled back briefly, then relaxed. To Maude and Hetty, the world was cloaked in silence, a stark contrast to the chaos gripping the town.

Quietly, patiently, Maude waited, giving Hetty whatever time she needed as the wagon continued on.

They pulled up in front of the bank, but still Hetty remained motionless. As they sat there, the body of the dead woman passed by, draped with a blanket.

A breeze, along with a hole in the road allowed a glimpse of a bare arm and bloated face. There was a cut across the forehead and shoulder. At the sight, Hetty let out a whimper, hiding her face in Maude's shoulder.

Seeing the dead woman bothered Maude, but at Hetty's reaction, Maude hugged the younger woman tighter. Maude watched as Doc Brown re-covered the body. They were taking it to his office for examination.

"Hetty," Maude murmured, "Hetty, what's wrong?"

Clover squirmed and then jumped down from the wagon seat, tying the horse to the post in front of the bank. Otherwise, silence reigned at the back of the wagon.

Maude and Hetty stirred. She looked at Maude, her eyes haunted.

"I'm sorry," Hetty said, straightening up. "Shall we head into the bank?"

"Ya've nothin' to be sorry for," Maude assured Hetty. "Sure yer okay? We kin wait."

"I'm fine," Hetty said, giving Maude a wan smile.

Leaving the back of the wagon, Maude joined Clover as Hetty went into the bank.

Approaching the teller, Hetty asked, "May I write a

draft on my bank in St. Louis?"

The teller took in Hetty's attire, her pale face. To him she looked like one of the consumptives who were coming to the area in droves. Still, it was his job, so he smiled, "Of course, how much will the draft be for?"

"One hundred."

The teller gulped. It wasn't an excessive amount, but he wasn't sure about Hetty. He passed her the paperwork. As she began filling it out, he asked, "You moving from St. Louis?"

"No, I live in Kiowa Wells. My return trip was delayed. I'm on my way back," Hetty answered, smiling as she handed the draft back to the man.

"It will only be a minute," the teller said, "I just need to clear it with the president."

Hetty smiled, "Fine, could you tell me where the telegraph office is? I want to send a telegram to Marshal Murphy in Kiowa Wells to let he and his wife know I'm on my way home."

At the mention of the Marshal's name, the teller paused, then proceeded to the president's office. He returned quickly and counted out Hetty's money.

"Hope you have a safe trip," the teller offered as Hetty prepared to leave. "And the telegraph office is three blocks down and one block toward the river. Train station is right next door."

"Thank you again," Hetty replied as she walked by the man who'd followed her in. There was something familiar about him, Hetty thought, then dismissed it as a reaction to the shock she'd suffered earlier. She realized she probably owed Maude an explanation, but she'd been so shocked by the events she couldn't talk about it. It brought back memories, some still at the forefront of her mind, after the run-in with Boggs.

Gone was the whimsy, the joy, the cheer she and Maude shared on their trip to town. Now, Hetty felt compelled to warn Maude of what Boggs had done, her role in his initial incarceration and what he was capable of. But it needed to be done in a way to drive home how truly dangerous the man was.

# CHAPTER
## *Twenty - Four*

**W**arner signaled the bartender who quickly came over with a bottle and two glasses. Lifting the bottle Warner said, "From my private stock." Pouring a drink for himself and Grant, Warner raised his glass, "Here's to your good health, and I have to admit I admire your style, Davis."

Grant had just lifted his own glass, but at Warner's words his neck muscles tensed. Not wanting to give away the fact he wondered how Warner knew his name, Grant nodded, "And to your good health, too."

Warner smiled, drawing his pistol, pointing it straight at Grant. "You must have a death wish Davis, or you're better with the gun than anybody expects."

Grant slowly replaced his glass on the bar. While his stomach muscles tightened, he did his best to relax, turning slightly to lean his back against the bar. Glancing behind and in front he saw at least two others who had him boxed in. "What's this all about?"

Warner's laugh, genuine humor flashing in his eyes. "You mean you don't know?"

"What's there to know?" Grant answered. "All I wanted was to see if I could locate Swisher. You said he wasn't here, so what else is there to know?" While Grant had been talking, he took in the rest of his surroundings. If anyone else in the saloon knew what was going on, they were choosing to ignore it.

"You really don't know, do you?" Warner said. "You're worth five thousand dollars—dead."

"Really? News to me," Grant shrugged, raising his hand to push his hat back.

"You're taking it mighty well."

"Well, considering you've got a gun on me, and there are two others who have me boxed. No use to fight what can't be stopped," Grant said, as his hand continued upward. He grabbed his hat, swinging it at Warner, and lowering his right shoulder, hit the startled man in front of him. Grant then swerved around him, past Warner, making for the back door. He'd just burst through as the bullets started to fly. Turning quickly to the left, he headed down a dark alley. He heard shouts of pursuit behind him. Warner's voice carried above all the rest, "Any man plugs him, I'll pay an extra five hundred." With those words, Grant knew he was a dead man if he couldn't find a place to hide.

Turning left again, he ran behind the saloon and past the next two buildings. He made another quick left and slid around to the front corner of the building. He looked up and down the street. What he saw did not give him much hope. There were men running around, shouting and firing at any movement or shadow they saw. Grant wondered how many would be wounded or dead by the time the sun came up. He just prayed he wouldn't be one of them. With few options open to him, Grant stepped up onto the boardwalk walking slowly away, doing what he could to not draw attention.

There were so many people looking for him, some didn't even know what he looked like, he was able to make a couple of blocks, then he crossed the street. Once there, he returned the way he had come on the opposite side of the road. Another block, and Grant made a right turn into the alley. He felt his way along a wall and then felt the handle of a door under his hand. Trying the knob, he found it unlocked. Slipping inside, he closed the door softly behind him. He was in some kind of storeroom, so he stood still as his eyes adjusted to the darkness.

Grant heard the mob running and shouting outside. He figured he'd only bought himself a few minutes, but miracles happened in less, not that he was expecting one. Standing there, the brief respite giving him time to think. Nothing had come to him, but he wasn't ready to give up just yet.

As Grant's eyes adjusted, he could make out boxes, furniture, and other assorted pieces associated with a hotel. "Looks like you lucked onto the one place Warner can't control," he whispered as he continued his search around the perimeter of the room, being careful not to bump into anything.

He'd covered about two thirds of the area when he found another door. Hand on the knob, he paused. What right did he have to bring his trouble to strangers? He was turning away when he heard a woman's voice, "Garrett, go lock the outside storeroom door. I'll not have that mob comin' into my place."

Grant moved behind the door, just as it opened. A man stepped through carrying a lantern. Knowing he would probably be seen, Grant waited as the man locked the outside door. He stepped into the light as the man returned.

Pulling a knife, the man asked, "And just who would you be?"

Grant raised his hands, "I'm the one the mob's after."

The man glared at Grant, "So you—"

Grant interrupted, "Only wanted a moment to think, never intended to cause trouble for anyone. If I might stay a bit longer, then…"

"You're coming with me," the man pointed to the door he'd come through.

Grant could draw and fire, but he didn't want to kill anyone. He'd never shot in anger, and only killed once, in self-defense. That shooting still haunted him. In addition, the shot would only draw the very people he was trying to escape.

Shrugging his shoulders, Grant walked through the door the man indicated. They walked down the hall and into an office off the lobby, avoiding any windows along the way. As they stepped inside, the man behind him said, "Look what I found, ma'am."

A tall, statuesque white-haired woman turned from the window, where she'd been looking out the edge of the drawn shade.

"Says he's the one they're lookin' for."

"Is that true, are they looking for you?" The woman asked, her voice low, yet commanding. Despite his situation, Grant liked her. Whether she would like him, given the situation, was another thing.

"Yes, ma'am, they are looking for me. Name's Grant Davis"

"Why, what did you do?"

"Nothing. I'd gone into the saloon for information about a man I'm looking for. Next thing I know, I'm being offered a drink, with a side of bullets."

"I see. Did Warner have anything to do with your situation?"

Grant could see the woman truly seemed to care about his answers. "He's the one pulled the gun first. Then said something about me being worth five thousand dollars."

A knowing light flashed in the woman's eyes. "You can leave, Garrett. I'll be fine."

"Yes, ma'am. You want me to keep an eye outside and let you know..."

"Yes, please."

When Garrett had left, the woman indicated a chair next to the fireplace. Grant took it, while she sat in the other. "I'm Mrs. Smith, and I'd like to know if you know Vivian Davis?"

At the sound of his mother's name, Grant paused, his breath catching. If this woman knew his mother, then he needed to get out of here as quickly as possible before...

"Relax, I'm not turning you over to the mob," Mrs. Smith said. "Now, would you please answer the question."

"She's my mother."

"I see. She must really hate you."

"She does, but what has that to do with anything?"

Mrs. Smith sighed, giving Grant a sad look. "You really don't know, do you? Son, it was your mother who put the reward out for you."

Grant sat up straight, stomach clenching as if physically punched. He knew his mother wanted him out of her life, but this? His mind blanked, then memories flooded in. Events of that reality barging past the walls he put up to block out the pain of hate, of not being lovable. "I knew she hated me, but..." Grant said in a low, pain-filled voice.

Garrett stuck his head in the door, "They're heading this way."

Grant was struggling with Mrs. Smith's revelation, and came close to panic at Garrett's words.

"You wait here," Mrs. Smith ordered, then she reached over, patting his hand. "No need to panic." She proceeded out the door and to the entrance of the hotel.

Grant heard the noise of the crowd begin to subside. What a hold this woman must have that her mere presence quieted a crowd.

"Gentlemen," her voice carried, "why are you so intent on creating such a fuss? You should be settling into the comfortable warmth of your beds, which for some of you is the bottle."

Grant heard laughter then a voice shouted, "But, Warner promised five hundred dollars."

"You let us in," demanded another.

"You hidin' that man?" roared another voice.

Quietly, so quietly they had to quiet to hear her, Mrs. Smith addressed the crowd. "You will not enter the hotel and bother my guests any more than you already have. As for Warner, you know him. How many of you really think you'd actually see that five hundred?"

Grant listened to the sound of people moving away. His panic eased up. He was thankful for Mrs. Smith's help, but what future problems had he brought to her doorstep?

A man began shouting, "You can't stop me," and Grant's panic returned.

# CHAPTER
### Twenty-Five

G rant rose to make his escape. While he wanted to live, he wasn't willing be the cause of harm coming to anyone. Look what had happened to Hetty. He couldn't continue adding innocent people to his list. His hand was on the door knob when he heard, "You heard Mrs. Smith, you'll not be going in," followed by another voice, "Come on, I'll buy you a drink, man's probably left town."

The sounds of the crowd faded away. Grant let his hand fall away, as he let out the breath he'd been holding. Still he hesitated returning to his seat.

He was standing there by the door when Garrett walked in, followed closely by Mrs. Smith.

Seeing Grant, she smiled, "Preparing your escape?"

"I didn't want you to be made out to be a liar, or have anyone here hurt on account of me."

Mrs. Smith smiled, "I never said you weren't here. I

said they couldn't come in."

"But…"

Turning to Garrett, Mrs. Smith directed, "We need to move his horse."

"You did come in by horse didn't you?"

"Yes ma'am, but it's horses."

"Horses?" Repeated Mrs. Smith as she raised an eyebrow. "I assume they are in the street?"

"Actually, the livery."

Clapping her hands Mrs. Smith said, "Even better, the hostler stays nearby and eats a few meals here."

"Be careful with Odysseus," Grant told Garrett. Then he added "He's a bit skittish and doesn't like other riders. It's my wife's horse."

Nodding, Garrett left and Mrs. Smith turned curious eyes toward Grant. "Wife?"

*Why did you mention wife*, Grant thought. *It will only complicate an already strange situation.* Of course, he wasn't sure Hetty thought of their marriage as the real thing. "It's complicated," Grant answered.

"We've some time before things calm down enough for you to leave," Mrs. Smith said. "Why don't you tell me your story, including your wife?"

Grant wasn't sure he cared to tell his whole story. Still, Mrs. Smith seem truly interested. He hesitated still, "I don't want to keep you from your work or your rest."

A knowing smile showed in Mrs. Smith's eyes. "It might help, and I'm a good listener."

"First, I have to ask," Grant began, not sure how to proceed. Taking a deep breath, he continued, "How, or do you, really know my mother?"

"Don't really know her, but I know of her. In my business you hear things," she answered, "and all of the information about her hasn't been good. The reward, the similarity of names, it all caught my attention."

Liking the woman's calm interest and the help she'd offered set Grant at ease. He began talking, and once started, the floodgates opened. Grant told about his father, how his mother changed even more with the death of her first son. His voice a combination of hurt and anger when he spoke of how his brother had betrayed him and his time in prison. He told of his search for Swisher and his part in the betrayal. He talked of the letter that brought Hetty into his life, Boggs and their strange marriage. By the time he finished, the town had quieted down. Looking at his rescuer, Grant was surprised at her continued interest. He must've been talking for a couple of hours. Mrs. Smith had nodded, commented a couple of times. Her questions helped keep him talking. Now she nodded wisely.

"I'm not one to give advice, son, but I'm surprised you didn't let this Hetty go when you two escaped from Boggs. By the way, as you know, Boggs is a nasty piece of work."

"So I found out. I'd just wanted to find Swisher, then I hooked up with him hoping to save my wife, now..."

"And now you still have your wife's prize horse? From what you said, that horse is very special, and not only to your wife." When Grant would have interrupted, Mrs. Smith held up a hand. "Grant, you pretty much slapped her in the face when you burned that letter. I would have left you then and there, especially if I'd risked my life to get it to you."

Grant hadn't thought of that. He'd been so focused on himself, on his quest. "But, why didn't she?" He whispered to himself, but it seems Mrs. Smith heard his last statement.

"Maybe for the same reason you keep a piece of her with you," Mrs. Smith paused, then very gently she added, "You care for her and I believe she cares for you."

"How could she care about me, an outlaw?"

"Maybe an outlaw to those who don't know, but if I were you, I'd go back to my wife and find out how she really feels. Burdens are somewhat easier when shared."

Grant saw understanding, yet pain in the woman's eyes. Was that pain for him, or for herself? "You might be right.

As soon as it's safe, I think I'll follow your advice."

"I hope you find the answer you want, and I pray you both will survive and thrive through all of this. Now, it's getting late and we have your escape to arrange."

Grant stood when Mrs. Smith rose. "Stay here. Garrett will get you when it is safe," she said, leaning in to give Grant a hug and a kiss on the cheek. "Let me know if you can, how it all turns out."

"I will," Grant said to the closing door.

# CHAPTER
*Twenty-Six*

A fter paying for her ticket, Hetty sent a wire to Marshal Murphy, following up on the letter she'd sent. Then she sent another wire to US Marshal Wright, also from Kiowa Wells.

"Maude," Hetty said, taking the older woman's hand, "Please take this to help pay for a tutor of your choice."

Maude pulled against Hetty's hold on her hand, but at Hetty's words, relaxed. "Where shall I send those letters?" Maude asked.

"In care of general delivery, Kiowa Wells, Colorado. They'll make sure I receive them, no matter where I am," Hetty smiled, giving Maude a huge hug.

When Hetty released her, Maude opened her hand, eyes growing wide. She gasped, then cast Hetty a questioning look, "Fifty dollars?"

Hetty nodded. Changing the subject, Hetty asked, "Where can I find the police station?"

"We'll take ya, but...," Maude answered as the two started walking back to the wagon.

"I'll explain to you and the police the same time," Hetty interrupted. "It's not something I want to talk about or repeat too many times. I hope you understand."

They walked the rest of the way in silence. Maude told Clover to head the wagon to the police station. The remainder of the trip was silent as Maude kept a careful eye on Hetty.

As Clover exited the wagon, Hetty turned toward him, "I'd like for you to come in with us." Hetty turned to Maude adding, "Please, I need you and Clover to believe all I'm going to say."

The three entered the police office, taking a seat, waiting for one of the officers to return. Maude looked at Hetty, sitting ramrod straight, eyes focused at the wall in front of them. Maude worried about Hetty, but sensed this was something Hetty was determined to see through.

They didn't have long to wait before an officer came in and, seeing the three asked, "What can I do for you?"

Hetty turned toward the man. Rising she extended her hand saying, "My name is Harriet Osgood," she paused not sure about adding her outlaw husband's name. She mentally shrugged, then continued, "Davis. I have some information that you may find useful."

"Useful in what way?" the officer asked.

"It's information from my past, that may have an impact in the investigation regarding the dead woman you found in the river."

At the mention of the body, the officer looked closer at Hetty. "Let me get the Marshal, I'm sure he'll want to hear this. Would you mind continuing to wait?" The man asked as he headed out the door.

Hetty remained standing. Both Maude and Clover shared a questioning look.

Seeing the look, Hetty gave them a weak smile saying, "Please be patient."

Maude nodded, glancing at her son, who nodded his agreement.

Within five minutes the deputy returned, with an older man they assumed was the Marshal. Their assumption was confirmed as the man walked over to Hetty offering his hand, "I am Marshal Harris. I understand you have some information?"

"I believe I do."

"Why don't you tell me what you know, " the Marshall said. "If you'll have a seat, we can get started."

"This all began some time ago when I was a child of about twelve," Hetty began, after seating herself. "First, let me ask you Marshal, have you heard of a man named Conover Boggs?"

"No, but I do know that there's a family of Boggs southeast of here."

"Mr. Boggs killed a young woman back in Kentucky, and I saw the body," Hetty said, her eyes focusing on the Marshal as she gripped the edge of her chair. "I testified against him, and he was sent to prison, swearing that if he ever found me, he would kill me."

"I can see how that would be terrifying, but what does that have to do with the dead woman we have here?"

"Conover Boggs is in this area, and the marks on the dead woman you have here are very similar to the ones on the woman back in Kentucky."

All eyes were on Hetty. Her mind saw again the attack she had witnessed as a child, and the subsequent terrors from testifying. The silence continued until the Marshal asked, "And how do you know that this Conover Boggs is in this region?"

This was the part Hetty had wanted to avoid, but knew that she needed to tell the truth. Taking a deep breath, Hetty looked down at her hands, then up at the Marshal.

"I ran into Conover Boggs in Pueblo, and he would have killed me if my husband, Grant Davis, had not convinced him that he had the wrong person.

Unfortunately, Boggs forced my husband and me to travel with him, I think in the hopes that he could prove that Grant had lied. We managed to escape two days later, but Boggs is tracking Grant, and I'm sure has someone following me in the hopes of eliminating both of us."

Maude reached over, taking one of Hetty's hands into hers. "Yer husband told me 'bout Boggs, I'd no idea."

Both the Marshal and his deputy were staring at Hetty.

The Marshal asked gently, "Did your husband know about this—your connection to this Boggs?"

"I had hinted at it, but he didn't know the whole story."

"I understand," the Marshal said. "You're a very lucky woman to have a husband who cares so much for you."

In her heart, Hetty wished what the Marshal said was true. What was true was Grant was a good man, and she was going to do everything she could to help him get his life and reputation back. She hopefully had set things in motion when she sent the packet back to Kiowa Wells. However, this was not the time to bring up his past since the Marshal said nothing about it.

So deep in thought about Grant, she almost missed the Marshal's next question.

"Do you have any idea where this Boggs might be?"

"Grant was heading north and west when I became ill and was left with Maude and her son. Other than that, I am not sure where he would be now."

"Well that's a start, would you mind giving me a description, and we will keep a lookout for this Boggs," the Marshal said. "Deputy, would you head over to Doc's and let him know I'll be by for his findings in a bit?"

The deputy left, and Hetty, gave the Marshal a description of Boggs.

When she finished, the Marshal said, "Thank you. Will you be around in case we catch him?"

Maude quickly answered, "Hetty's on 'er way back ta Kiowa Wells, but me an' Clover live jest north an' west o' town. Ya call on us if'n ya need to."

"Thank you, and I hope you have a safe journey, Mrs. Davis."

As the three left the police station, Hetty turned toward Maude saying, "Before I leave, I'd like to see the prison. I realize it might not be a place you want to visit but..."

Maude stared at Hetty, "Ya sure?"

"Maude, I need to see where Grant was. I want to try to understand as best I can."

Maude nodded, "Boggs fit inta this, too?"

Hetty paused, thinking about Maude's question. "I realize Colorado's different from Kentucky, but you may have something there."

"What I can't understand is how he got out?" Hetty continued. "When I saw him, I thought I was seeing things."

"If'n what ya told the Marshal is true, I think we're needin' ta be mighty careful," Maude replied.

"We do, and I'm worried he may come back and harm you and Clover."

"If'n yer worried, don't. We'll be jest fine," Maude answered Hetty, then added, "prison is on the far west end. We kin drive by that way, to give ya a bit more time afore you leave."

"Thank you. I'll try not to take too long."

The three headed toward the prison, a man shadowing their movements, but no one took notice.

# CHAPTER
*Twenty - Seven*

Pulling up about a hundred yards away from the prison wall, Hetty climbed down from the wagon, walking slowly forward. She took in the wall, built by the inmates she had been told, the three-story stone building where the prisoners were housed. There were men in the yard, their striped clothing marking them as criminals, along with armed guards watching them.

How did Grant survive? Hetty thought. To be confined, having to live by someone else's schedule. All these thoughts tumbled through Hetty's mind. She wasn't sure she'd ever understand. At the same time she was thankful Grant had kept that concern for others. Where would she be now if he'd become hardened, jaded with the world, from having spent time behind the these walls. What of Maude's husband? How would his time here change him?

Turning away, Hetty returned to the wagon where

Maude and Clover waited.

"Thank you," Hetty began, "I know—"

"Don't ya let it bother ya," Maude interrupted. "My husband only has a few more months. Moved here ta be close jest in case—" Maude paused, then smiled. "In the meantime I've my memories."

Hetty watched Maude as her eyes became unfocused, a smile on her face. Would she ever have that kind of joy with Grant? For that matter would she ever see him again?

"Maude," Hetty whispered, "I hope you can make even better memories soon."

"If'n you an' Grant 'ave half as much feelin' fer each other as we did, ya'll be mighty lucky."

Hetty couldn't let herself believe that, but given a chance, she would love to try. Instead of words, Hetty grinned. Then realizing how much time had passed, she said, "I think we'd better head to the station. As much as I'd love to remain here, I've got things to get done."

Maude nodded and they climbed back into the wagon, heading east to the train station. They pulled up just as the train pulled in.

"Made it," Maude grinned.

"I…" Hetty began, then pulling Maude into a hug, "I look forward to those letters."

"Ye'll get 'em."

Fighting tears, Hetty walked toward the station. "Be safe, and thank you for everything," she called back over her shoulder.

Both Maude and Clover waved, watching as Hetty boarded the train, followed by her shadow.

As the train traveled east, Hetty started going through her list of things she hoped to accomplish once she'd returned to Kiowa Wells.

First and foremost, of course, was to find a way to help Grant clear his name. She was thankful for all the supportive friends she'd made in the town. She knew the tight-knit community had weathered many changes, trials, and come out stronger than before.

Watching out the window, she pondered the early settlers who'd lived on these plains, foothills and mountains. She thought of where her place in that history might be. Would it be as a single schoolteacher her parents always told her she'd be, or would she actually find a shared happiness with someone?

Smiling a sad smile, she took herself to task for dwelling on things that were beyond her control. It would be better to focus on what was at hand, what was important in this moment. As the train pulled into the station at Pueblo, Hetty collected her belongings, and headed to the end of the car. She disembarked and walked to the station. There was to be a short wait before she caught the train going north.

Despite trying, Hetty couldn't sit still. Now with her health returning she was anxious to do what she'd set out to do. She'd already delivered the letter to Grant. That it wasn't a pile of ash was a miracle. Thinking of his reaction when she'd handed him letter, Hetty headed toward the telegraph office.

Walking in, she asked the operator "Can I send a wire to Marshal Murphy in Kiowa Wells?"

"If you write it down, I'll do what I can. There's been some trouble with the fires in the mountains and the winds out east," the operator replied.

Filling out the form she wrote "What have you learned?" H.

The operator took the form, counting said "That'll be two bits."

Handing the man the requested funds, Hetty said, "I've about two hours before the train leaves. Hopefully I'll be able to get an answer before then."

Hetty walked out, looking southward to where it all began. So much had happened since that fateful night. How would it all end, Hetty wondered? Would she ever see Grant again and if she did, what would happen? So many questions, but for now, Hetty would do what she could to help her husband as best she could.

# CHAPTER
*Twenty-Eight*

I t was about two hours before dawn when Garrett came back to get Grant. The night had been stressful, with Grant pacing the room Mrs. Smith had left him in. Still, he was tired enough, he'd found himself dozing off when he would sit in one of the chairs, only to wake up feeling panicked and closed in. It was almost a relief when Garrett came to the door saying, "Follow me."

The two walked through the hotel, arriving at a back door. Garrett held up his hand. He opened the door, and glanced out. Seeing nothing, he motioned Grant forward, and the two made their way to the stable. Grant found Odysseus and his horse, Nelly, saddled and ready to go.

"Thank you," Grant said offering his hand to Garrett. "Thank Mrs. Smith for me. Hope nothing bad happens to her because of this."

"You needn't worry about Mrs. Smith, I'll take care of

her," Garrett said, returning Grant's handshake. "Now, I think it'd be best if you got started. Most of the mob have either gone home or are passed out drunk, but be careful."

Nodding his head, Grant mounted up on Odysseus. Taking Nelly's reins from Garrett's hand, he exited the stable. Heeding Garrett's direction, Grant headed for the street behind the saloon, taking a route least expected. As he passed the saloon he saw the young cowboy, and the girl with the gaudy jewelry, climbing out an upstairs window, It looked like he had two friends below, on lookout. Grant moved on, hoping the quartet wouldn't see him. Unfortunately, that was not the case. The cowboy, riding double with his girl and their friends boxed him in.

"We saw you with Warner," the young cowhand started.

"Well, then you know that he's looking for me." Grant placed his hand on his pistol, as he continued. "If you think you're going to take me…" After a long and frustrating night, Grant was not going to be taken to Warner.

"The only place you're going is with us," one of the other two said.

"Why?" Grant asked. He wanted to get away and back to Hetty. In addition, the longer they sat here, the more chance all of them had of being seen, despite the hour.

"We can't have you telling what you saw," the third man said. "Sam and Constance here are going to get married and we don't want Warner or his men trying to stop it."

"You have nothing to worry about with me," Grant assured the quartet.

"No we won't, because you're coming with us." Sam said. "Nothing is going to stop us getting married."

Realizing to cause a fuss would only result in his getting caught, Grant acquiesced and then looking at Sam and Constance said, "Constance would you like to ride my extra horse, Nelly?"

Constance looked to her soon-to-be husband, and with a nod from him she said, "Thank you."

Sam rode over to Nelly, mounting the horse leaving Constance to ride his. Watching Sam, Grant smiled to himself. It seemed obvious Sam was very much in love with his young lady. He applauded the young cowhand's willingness to overlook the reputation of what most would say was a fallen woman. Seeing the two together, made him think of Hetty and their brief time together.

With Grant in tow, the quartet rode northwest out of town. He wondered where they were headed. When they turned south, Grant thought they might be heading toward Gunnison. The sun was lighting the eastern sky when they halted at a tiny shack on the outskirts of a small settlement. Looking over at Constance, Sam asked, "You sure this is what you want?"

"With all my heart."

Sam helped Constance down, and with the other two cowhands, walked over and knocked on the door. Glancing back, Sam said, "You've come this far with us, and we appreciate your offer of the extra horse," then in an embarrassed tone continued, "We'd like to have you witness our vows."

Grant looked at the two and their friends. With a shrug he dismounted, walking over to join the group as they entered the shack.

Within minutes, the justice of the peace was going through the ceremony. Grant thought how different it was from the one that Boggs had forced on him and Hetty. Where there it was a stand of trees and a bunch of outlaws. Here, he knew these two were doing it right.

Thinking of Hetty, Grant began to have his doubts. What did he really have to offer her? He was an outlaw, and unless he was able to clear his name, there was nothing, no future for her with him. He supposed he should be happy that although legal, their marriage was a sham. But in reality the thought of not having Hetty in his life made him feel sad.

Before he knew it, the new couple had said their 'I do's', and were smiling and kissing. Their friends hugging Constance and slapping Sam on the back. Grant stood off to the side, hat in hand, slowly working his fingers around the outside of the brim. What would he do now?

As if the others had heard his question, they all turned, looking at Grant, Sam and Constance smiled. "We appreciate that you didn't raise a fuss," Constance began.

Sam continued, "We mistook you. We're sorry if we kept you." Sam stopped, turning red at the memory of last night.

Grant smiled at the couple, "I wish you both the best. It's pretty obvious you care a great deal for each other. May you have a long and happy life together."

The two beamed even more at Grant, with Constance impulsively hugging him. "Where was you headed when we..." Sam began, his face turning even redder.

"I was heading out to try and avoid the mob, and get back to the person I care about." As Grant said it, he realized it was the truth. He wanted to get back to Hetty, convince her to stay with him while he worked to try to clear his name. It was more about making her life better than for himself. If she were beside him, he would succeed, he just knew it.

Mounting up, Grant pointed Odysseus south when Sam brought Nelly over. "Don't forget your other horse."

Turning, Grant looked at the couple and their friends. Sam continued, "We can get a horse here, you may need Nelly when you find the person you're looking for."

Grant smiled, and reaching down, took Nelly's reins from Sam. With a nod to the young people, he turned south again. He wasn't sure where he was going. He wasn't sure where Hetty might be, or if she were alive, but he had to start somewhere. He thought he'd start at Maude's. Hetty might still be there, and if not, Maude might know where she had gone.

The thing he needed to worry about was staying out of overly-populated areas. If his mother had put the price on his head, he needed to be extra vigilant.

# CHAPTER
## *Twenty-Nine*

O nce out of sight of the small settlement, Grant turned, heading east. Grant hoped to bypass any towns as he headed east toward Canon City and Hetty. If he could make Tin Cup pass without getting too close to the town he'd so recently escaped, he could head down to the St. Elmo area, then swing a bit south. From there, he should be able to follow the Arkansas to Maude's place.

Staying just south of Virginia City, Grant managed to get past without being seen. He thought about stopping by Molly's place, but the thought of seeing Hetty drove him forward.

"With any luck, Odysseus, you'll see your mistress soon," Grant told the horse as they started down the east side of the pass.

Odysseus shook his head. Grant laughed, a sound he found odd. But the laughter released tension he hadn't realized he was carrying. He tried to think how Hetty would respond to all that had happened to him since they'd parted. He'd laughed when they'd been trying to fool Boggs, but it wasn't the happy laugh he'd just had.

As if wanting to be part of what Grant and Odysseus were sharing, Nelly trotted closer, nudging Grant's leg.

Turning, Grant reached over and petted Nelly's neck. "Yes, you'll be carrying me into who knows what soon enough."

Nelly shook her mane and tail, like she was frustrated. "Okay," Grant said, dismounting and switching saddles.

About two miles down the pass, Grant saw smoke. Not the smoke of a campfire, but what appeared to be a forest fire where they were headed.

Grant realized he was in trouble. Flames were racing toward him, driven by an eastern wind. With luck, if he headed north, they might be able to ride out past the edge of the flames.

Kicking his heels into Nelly's flanks, Grant and the two horses shot north. He kept looking to his right, realizing—despite the effort—they were not going to make it. Then, when he thought Nelly could run no faster, Odysseus nipped her and with a burst of speed the three managed to get out to the edge of the fire. Easing up, Grant let the horses set their own pace. As long as the wind didn't shift, Grant felt they might be safe.

"That was close," Grant breathed, as heat from the fire began to fade away the further north they rode. They had been lucky, but now he was way off course, cut off from the direction he'd been heading.

Grant watched the sky darken, except for the light from the fire. He knew he and the horses needed a break, but there would be no stopping this close to the flames.

Grant slowed down to a walk. He wanted to conserve the horses' energy, in case the fire turned and they needed another burst of speed. The trio continued on through the night, past the magic hour of nighttime and watched the mind-blowing beauty of the smoke-filled sunrise.

With the bulk of the fire finally behind him, Grant began hunting for a place to stop. The horses needed a rest, and he could use a couple hours of sleep.

An hour later, Grant found what he was looking for, an oasis away from the heat and flames. Unsaddling, he let the horses roll, giving each some water from his canteen before he picketed them on the grass.

Grant leaned back against a pine, falling into an exhausted sleep. The sun filtered down through the smoke and trees, warming Grant's tired muscles.

To Grant, it seemed only minutes before he was pulled awake by the horses. They were fussing and trying to pull away.

"What is it?" Grant asked, jumping up to secure the two. He looked around for what might have scared them. His first thought was he'd been followed, but discarded the thought. Neither horse was the kind to panic if someone were nearby. They would let him know, but not try to run away. He didn't see any wild animals nearby.

Since he was awake, Grant thought he might as well move on. Still puzzled, he continued watching the surrounding area while saddling Odysseus. He had just finished when he heard a growl and a rustling in the brush behind him.

Whirling, he caught sight of a singed mountain lion flying toward him. There was no time to mount and ride away. He started to draw his pistol, but the scared animal landed on him before he'd cleared his holster. The lion's claws raked his shoulders, it's teeth mere inches from his face.

Putting up his arms to protect his face, he felt the rear claws sink through his pants and into his thighs. Visions of Hetty flashed through his mind as he struggled to throw the animal from him.

"No," he growled, "I can't be this close to finding what I want only to lose now." He gathered his strength, pushing upward. Despite his effort he'd only managed to get his hands under the chin of the animal, barely escaping the second bite. The animal raked it's claws across his chest and legs as it tried to get at Grant's throat.

Grant knew he was in a fight for his life, one he might lose. A part of his brain understood the big cat was scared and fighting for its own life. The fire had driven it his way, but he didn't want to die out here in the middle of nowhere. He didn't want to die without seeing Hetty again.

Suddenly the weight of the lion flew off Grant. The big cat growled, but took off running. Grant saw Odysseus chasing and nipping at the fleeing animal.

Grant rolled over and by the time Odysseus returned, he was standing, barely. Coming over to Grant, Odysseus nuzzled Grant's shoulder, then pulled back as he caught the smell of blood.

Grant caught at the reins, and pulling the horse closer, leaned with his hands over the saddle. Grant heaved a scared breath. "Thanks boy."

Mounting up, Grant went to find Nelly, who'd bolted off. Swaying with shock and pain, Grant soon found Nelly pulling up tufts of grass. As Grant rode up, Nelly lifted her head, trotting over like she was glad to see her owner.

Leaning over to grab the reins, Grant almost fell from the saddle. He secured Nelly's reins to the saddle. He struggled but managed to regain his balance. The trio started out, heading northeast, farther from the receding flames.

"Looks like we're a bit off course," Grant mumbled. He'd not wanted to go to Leadville, but it was close. The way he was feeling, he knew he needed help. Somewhere along the way, Grant tied his wrists to the pommel to keep from falling off, should he pass out. He'd have to trust the horses to get him to where he needed to go.

# CHAPTER
*Thirty*

B
y the time Hetty's train was ready to leave, she'd not gotten an answer to her telegram. She asked the operator to pass on any message that came in for her to the office in Colorado Springs, her next stop. For an extra charge, the man agreed.

Hetty boarded the train, finding a seat near the back of the car. Taking a window seat, she settled in for the next leg of her journey. She could have gone east from Pueblo, but decided to go to Colorado Springs. From there she could either continue on the train to Denver, or take the stage east toward home.

She'd picked up the local paper to help take her mind off Grant and what might be happening to him. That she was worried had become painfully obvious to her. She shook her head, pulling the paper out she perused its pages, looking at the news for the area.

One of the first things to catch her eye was the

indictments of the County Treasurer and the County Commissioner in the town of Deadwood. The article also noted that as soon as three others were found, indictments would be handed down for them also. Hetty could never understand people like that. It made her even more grateful for the good friends and officials in the town of Kiowa Wells.

On the next page, Hetty read a short piece about a man who'd beaten his wife rather severely, and then took a pistol and shot himself in the heart. The story shocked Hetty. That the man had beaten his wife was all too common for some couples, as she had seen in her life. What surprised her, was that in his remorse, he would shoot himself. As shocking and sad as the story was, it made her wonder what it would be like to be truly married to Grant. The short time she had been with him, he'd been all that was kind and caring, despite the circumstances they'd found themselves.

Staring out the window, she noticed a herd of horses running through a pasture. She found herself mourning the loss of Odysseus. Yet, she was comforted by the fact he was with Grant. If anyone, anyone other than herself, were to be taking care of Odysseus, she wanted it to be Grant. In her heart of hearts, she truly did believe he was a good man despite the label of outlaw that had been handed him.

Thoughts of Grant both hurt and made her feel good at the same time. She wondered if she would ever see him again.

"Stop it," a child's voice broke through Hetty's thoughts. Glancing up from her paper, Hetty saw two children halfway up the car fussing with each other. The boy was pulling the girl's pigtails, and the girl was fighting back. The altercation brought a smile to Hetty's face, making her think of her students back at her school. She watched the woman, who appeared to be the children's mother, reprimand the two who lapsed into silence.

Hetty continued to watch the two children as they stuck their tongues out at each other, while trying hard to behave. It looked like a struggle they were losing. Watching the two, Hetty realized how much she enjoyed working with children. Watching their eyes light up when they got something right, seeing the concentration when they were trying to learn. Hetty wondered how she could give that up? This sudden marriage, regardless of how it ended, had put her job in jeopardy. Would she be able to continue teaching, a job she felt she was meant to do, if she never saw Grant again?

Hetty wasn't sure what she would do. A part of her wanted to be married, perhaps because she had always thought she never would be. She knew for a fact she was not attractive. Her parents had told her often enough. Even Grandmams had hinted at that truth. But when she was working with the children, she felt useful, proud of what she could impart to them. She truly believed she'd been born to be a teacher. Now, she might be faced with the choice. *No*, Hetty shook her head, it was not a choice. She would do what she could to help Grant get his life back, then she would return to hers.

"Next stop Colorado Springs," the conductor said as he walked through the car. Hetty folded her paper and gathering up the saddlebags, she prepared herself to disembark. Looking down at the dress Maude had fitted for her, she thought how incongruous she must look. With her hair tied back, and old-fashioned bonnet, a dress with lace and saddlebags. She'd never considered herself a fashionable woman, but she had to laugh at how she must look.

As the train pulled into the station, the two children and their mother hurried to disembark. Glancing out the window, she saw the woman and her children greeted by a man who despite the public place made known his joy at seeing them. It tugged at Hetty's heart to see a family so happy.

Stepping onto the platform, Hetty immediately went in search of the telegraph office to see if she'd received any answers to the message she'd sent.

Hetty was pleased there was an answer waiting for her. She felt she could relax, take in the show, "Bartholomew's School of Educated Horses and Performing Goats" before catching a stage to Kiowa Wells tomorrow. She'd missed the one o'clock show, but there was a repeat show at seven.

Walking back toward the train station, Hetty came across three men harassing a Chinaman. Placing her response in her saddle bag, Hetty approached the four men.

"What do you think you are doing?" Hetty demanded of the aggressors.

One of the group turned to look at her, commenting, "This ain't none of your concern."

"I beg to differ," Hetty responded, continuing, "Three against one should always be someone's concern."

The man who'd spoken turned and approached Hetty, his eyes angry. "I said it was none of your concern."

Hetty stood her ground, taking the saddlebags from her shoulder, "I suggest you leave the gentleman alone."

The man approached even closer hand raising to strike. Hetty took the saddlebags, swinging with all her might, knocking the man to the ground. Standing over him she said, "You are not much of a man are you? Not only do you fight unfairly making it three on one, you also think it is acceptable to attack women."

Hetty's actions were starting to bring a crowd. Out of that crowd stepped a police officer saying, "What's going on here?"

As the man was rising from the ground his two compatriots ceased their harassment, taking off. "Those three men were attacking the Chinaman, and when I asked them what they were doing they threatened me. Since I don't threaten easily, I hit this one with my saddlebags."

"That's a mighty dangerous thing for you to do ma'am," the officer said, a smile playing at his lips, "but I applaud your sense of duty."

"Do you need me for anything?" Hetty asked, "I have a stage to catch."

"No, I'll take care of it."

The Chinaman, who'd been the victim, came over to Hetty, and bowing low said," Thank you."

Hetty looked at the man and smiled, "What are we here for, if not to care for our fellow man?" At which point Hetty turned and continued on her way to the train station. The Chinaman fell into step beside her, not saying anything, but escorting her toward the station.

The closer they got to the station, the louder the noise became. Hetty realized that there were three or four other people harassing the passengers. As if on cue the Chinaman, fear in his eyes, nodded to Hetty and took off back the way he'd come.

Sighing, Hetty continued toward the station, realizing this was more than she could handle. She could not stop all of these attacks. Still she could help one or two. Walking forward, each step placed firmly on the ground, Hetty was close to the first perpetrator when she felt something push against her ribs. Before she could turn around, a voice whispered in her ear, "Kindly follow me and no one will get hurt."

Hetty tensed, hand moving toward the saddlebags when an arm went around her shoulder guiding her away from the train station and the activity there. "If you try anything, I'll not shoot you, but open fire on the people behind us."

Hetty didn't want the death or injury of innocent people on her head, so she did as she was bid. She was placed on a horse, her captor immediately swinging up behind her. They took off heading west. Hetty wondered what was going to happen next, but whatever it was, she would do her best to keep her wits about her. Hopefully she'd find a way out of the situation she found herself in.

Her captor did not stop as they made their way up the mountain pass. They climbed steadily to who knew where. Despite her strong constitution, Hetty found herself starting to sag. She realized her recent illness had taken more out of her than she'd thought. At some point, she must have passed out. She awoke in darkness, hands tied behind her, as they continued riding through the night.

# CHAPTER
## Thirty-One

Grant awoke, to see a face, surrounded by white and black. Beyond this vision he saw cots. He started to rise, but the pain in his shoulders and thighs, along with a gentle push, forced him back down.

"So you are finally awake," a female voice said.

"Where am I?"

"You are with the Sisters of Charity at their hospital in Leadville."

As his vision cleared, Grant realized he'd been looking into the kind face of a nun. He asked, "How did I get here?"

"One of the miners found you slumped over your horse, and brought you here."

"What became of my horses?"

"They are being cared for, they are safe." The woman said, her voice calm as she reached over to feel Grant's forehead. "You appear to be healing nicely, and your fever is gone."

"How long?"

"About thirty-six hours."

"I'm not sure how I can pay, but I will…" Grant began.

"We do not charge for helping our fellow man."

Grant laid back, tired but worried. The longer his journey was delayed, the greater the chance he wouldn't find Hetty. Somewhere within all his worries, plans, thoughts, Grant fell asleep.

The next time he opened his eyes, Grant felt much better. When he tried to rise there was some pain, but nothing he couldn't manage. Looking around, he saw one of the nuns caring for another patient. Rising, he padded over, asking, "May I ask where my things are? I feel I need to leave. I'm on an errand and need to get going."

"If you will give me a moment, I will get them for you," came the reply. "If you will have patience, I'll have another sister check your injuries before you leave."

Grant returned to his cot, easing himself down. His wait wasn't long. The sister returned quickly with his belongings. As he was being examined, they let him know where Odysseus and Nelly were being boarded.

"Sisters," Grant said as he was leaving, "When things get straightened out, I will remember what you have done, and return the favor for you to continue your work here."

Keeping his head down, Grant headed out, hoping to make the stables before anyone recognized him. His luck did not hold. Turning the last corner he ran into Joe "Frenchy" Brown. He tried to turn away before being spotted, but Frenchy hailed him. "Is that you, Davis?"

Seeing that it would be impossible to ignore the man, Grant pasted a smile on his face and answered, "Frenchy, when did you get out?"

"Two weeks ago. Imagine seeing you here," Frenchy said coming up to Grant and placing an arm around his shoulder. "Come with me and we will celebrate our freedom."

"I'd love to, but I have somewhere to be."

"Now you wouldn't be trying to run out on old Frenchy would you?" Frenchy said pulling Grant in even tighter.

Grant gritted his teeth as pain shot through his injured shoulders. He kept the smile on his face, hiding the injury. His time in prison taught him to not show pain in front of other prisoners, in case they used it against you. "Not at all," Grant replied, his smile growing even wider.

Grant remembered Frenchy and his unruly temper. There had been many a time in prison when Grant watched Frenchy get into fights, It didn't matter who it was, when his temper took over he'd fight with inmates or guards. After numerous times in isolation, he'd calmed down. Now, away from prison, Frenchy was reverting back to his old habits.

"I'd be glad to have one drink with you," Grant replied in the hopes of mollifying Frenchy's rising temper.

Slapping Grant on the back, he smiled. "I'm glad. Like for ya to meet my wife."

Grant was remembering the stories from other inmates who'd known Frenchy, and how jealous he became of anyone looking at his wife. If the man had only been out of prison for two weeks, Grant knew he was on tenuous ground when it came to Frenchy and his family. Letting himself be led, Grant soon found himself in front of a small house. A great deal of noise was coming from inside. Feeling his stomach knot up, Grant turned toward Frenchy saying, "Sounds like quite a time going on."

"What's the matter, old friend?"

"Well if you must know, I tangled with a mountain lion. Still dealing with some of the souvenirs it left me with." Grant finally said, holding his breath in hopes Frenchy wouldn't try something and open the still raw wounds.

"Well why didn't ya say so. I'll introduce ya to my wife, we'll have our drink, then you're free to go." Frenchy said magnanimously.

Grant wasn't sure he should believe Frenchy, but felt it better to go along. He could stay, have a drink, then leave as quickly as possible. Entering the house, Grant could see why so much noise was coming from inside. There were girls, rough looking men, and plenty of alcohol. A woman came up to Frenchy, giving him a kiss on the cheek, all the while eyeing Grant up and down.

"Who's this?" she purred.

Putting his arm around the woman, Frenchy pulled her close saying, "This here's Davis. We was in prison together."

"So you know my husband, I hope we can have a nice reunion," seduction in her voice.

"Yes ma'am," Grant said as he looked for a way to escape the situation that could go from bad to horrible in just a few seconds.

"Sorry, Davis, my wife, Anna."

Grant smiled at the woman. "Nice to meet you."

Pulling her husband close, kissing him soundly on the mouth. Anna turned toward Grant, linking her arm in his, pulling him further into the house.

"Let's have a drink to old friends, and new," Anna said as she poured drinks for herself, Grant, and Frenchy.

While Anna had a hold on him, she stroked his arm and shoulders. "You're quite a man. What were you in for?"

"They said I rustled some cattle."

"Did you always have these muscles, or did prison give them to you."

The look Frenchy gave him, made the hair on the back of Grant's head rise.

Pulling Anna with him, Grant poured himself a glass of liquor and with a shout called, "A toast, to an old friend and his wife, wishing them both the best, may you have a long and happy life." Grant downed the fiery liquid, feeling the burn all the way down.

Pulling Frenchy aside, Grant said, "Frenchy, you're a lucky man. I don't want to interfere with your homecoming. Catch you later." Grant turned, making his way out of the house and back to the stable.

He'd only gone a couple hundred yards when Swisher came up. "Well if it isn't Grant Davis."

"Swisher, I'd hoped I'd run into you again."

"Well, looks like I found you first. I have a message for you."

Grant tensed. He expected Swisher to either pull his gun or throw a punch. Instead Swisher held out a piece of paper. "I've been looking for you to deliver this. Now that it's delivered, I'll see you later."

Before Grant could react, Swisher faded into an alley. Grant could hear his steps running away. A part of him wanted to follow, for he had spent so long trying to find the man to clear his name. But as he felt the paper in his hand, along with Swisher's cryptic message, Grant let him go. Once in the stables, Grant opened the piece of paper, his hand's shaking.

The note read: *If ya want to see your wife again, you'll come to the old abandoned cabin shown on the map.* The note was signed *Boggs*, with a crude map drawn below the message.

Grant felt himself go cold, Boggs had Hetty. Mounting quickly, Grant, Odysseus, and Nelly took off to find Hetty and Boggs.

# CHAPTER
## Thirty-Two

T he open doorway taunted Hetty. It had been over thirty-six hours since Hetty had found herself in this remote mountain cabin. It was still dark when her kidnapper had ridden up. Hetty's heart almost jumped out of her chest when the man handed her off of the horse, directing her toward the cabin where Conover Boggs stood, lamp in hand.

"Did you have any trouble?" Boggs asked.

"She wanted to give me some trouble, but that didn't last long," the man said. Then as he gave Hetty a little shove toward Boggs, added, "Ain't that right, lady?"

"Ya did a good job," Boggs told the man. "Why don't you take a rest will I deal with the lady?"

The man walked off, taking the horse with him. Boggs grabbed Hetty, shoving her into the cabin. The sudden push, and with her hands tied behind her back, Hetty lost her balance landing hard on the cabin's dirt floor. Behind her she heard Boggs laugh uncontrollably.

"Well, ain't you the clumsy one?"

Hetty struggled to roll over, only to have Boggs grab her by the arm, jerking her upward. He held her face close to his. He had the lamp in one hand while the other tightly gripped her upper arm.

"Now, we'll see what you're worth."

Boggs thrust her into a straight-backed chair, securing her there. That was where she remained, except for those few times when Boggs or the other man escorted her out when necessary. So far she'd had no food, and just enough water to keep her from passing out.

Now, as Hetty stared out the window she still had not figured out the meaning of Boggs' comment about how much she was worth.

A storm had blown in, with lots of wind and rain. This left the high mountain air clear, a freshness to the look outside the door. To keep herself from worrying, Hetty wondered what it would be like to visit the end of a rainbow. She imagined a lush green valley, a ranch, herself and children. She imagined Grant riding up, a smile on his face as he rode in. He would pull her into his arms. "I love you wife," he'd say as he kissed her, a kiss that told Hetty he loved her more than anything in the world.

She was pulled from her imaginings as Boggs walked through the door. "Shouldn't be much longer."

Hetty glared at him, only to have him laugh in her face, as he raised a bottle of whiskey to his mouth

To Hetty's mind, Boggs was the worst kind of human. He seemed to take pleasure in tormenting her, knowing she couldn't leave; the ropes securing her had seen to that.

"Mighty pretty rainbow," his voice whispered in her ear. "I always loved rainbows."

"I don't believe you," Hetty spat. "How could someone who does what you do…"

"See, you judge so harshly," Boggs interrupted, adding, "Just so you know, I have you here so Grant will see you, so he knows…"

"Knows what? How do you know he's coming?"

Boggs didn't make sense. There was no convincing him that holding her hostage was a waste of time.

Hetty closed her eyes, shutting out the vision of freedom. What would Odysseus do in this situation, the hero she revered from Homer's Odyssey, Hetty wondered. "Who am I kidding, he would not be tied up in a mountain cabin."

She must've spoken out loud for the voice continued in her ear. "You never know, Grant could find himself in your situation, except I've found out he's worth a lot more dead."

At hearing Boggs' statement about Grant being worth more dead, Hetty started to panic. The more Boggs said, the more frightened Hetty became.

Boggs started laughing again, "If you don't get a hold of your fear you won't be able to help."

A hand came down on her shoulder, moving up to massage her neck. Hetty started to tense, but forced herself to relax under his hand. A chuckle reached her ear.

"Wise choice," Boggs sneered, his hand sliding forward, fingers caressing her throat. Just as quickly they tightened, cutting off her air supply. Hetty tried to break the hold, but the ropes held her tight.

"Just so's you know who's in control," Boggs snickered as his fingers let go. In the next breath, he asked her his own question, like the last few minutes hadn't happened. "So when did you two get married?"

The sudden change frightened Hetty even more. His constant change kept her off-balance. The more off-balance, the less—Hetty knew—she could help herself, let alone Grant. Hetty sighed softly. Perhaps she could play that game, too. "The Odyssey by Homer is my favorite. I've read portions to my students, before I married. I intend to pass that love of classics along to our children."

"So you were a teacher."

"Yes, I was a teacher," Hetty answered.

"You ever been kissed by someone other than that husband of yours?" Boggs whispered in her ear. She felt his breath against her cheek. She wanted to scream, run, but since that wasn't an option, her mind sought another tactic to alleviate the terror threatening her again.

"Yes," Hetty answered.

"So, you're a loose woman?"

"No, I wouldn't" Hetty began, only to scream as a slap stung her face.

"Yes, you are. You've been traveling alone with a man," he screamed. "I think you lied about being married, and that ceremony we performed was fake."

Hetty had heard enough. Then Boggs' words hit her. *The ceremony was a fake.* Did that mean Grant knew? She remembered he and Boggs talking, laughing. No, Hetty didn't think Grant knew. If he did, then why would he help her escape, and why kill Grant now? Her fear for herself retreated in the face of her anger. "I am married. You talked about judging, well you certainly don't practice what you..."

She was silenced as a hand covered her mouth, Boggs' breath caressing her hair. Hetty caught a glimpse of that hated face as his lips closed in. She wanted to get away, it was all too much. Everything went black as his fingers clamped her lips and nose. His laughter ringing in her ears.

# CHAPTER
## Thirty-Three

O utside of Leadville, Grant's emotions were much like the storm building to the west of him. He knew he was in for a difficult time, but foremost in his mind was Hetty. Was she really being held captive, or was this an ambush in the making?

Grant took stock of who knew of his and Hetty's relationship; of who wanted him dead for the money his mother had put on his head. It basically winnowed down to one person: Boggs.

If it was Boggs, Grant knew, unless he could find a way to stop it, both he and Hetty could end up dead.

Even without the reality of Hetty's past encounters with the outlaw, for Grant knew they hadn't really fooled the man, Boggs wouldn't leave a witness.

Grant's eyes grew misty or was it the clouds and wind that caused his eyes to water? Storms at these elevations could be horrific or die away. Either way the wind buffeted

Grant as he headed to his destination and to Hetty.

Slowly, Grant made his way south and east according to the map. Would he be able to outmaneuver a man as manipulative as Boggs? Could he find a way to save Hetty, if in fact Boggs had her?

As Grant thought through as many possible scenarios for the upcoming confrontation, one thing became perfectly clear, Hetty needed to live, no matter what the cost to him. Their marriage might have been a jest to Boggs. It was true, Grant in trying to save Hetty had set the stage. Now, for Grant, Hetty had become someone very important.

If they both survived, would they be able to make it a real marriage? Would it be one that would stand the test of time? Did he have what it took to be a good husband to someone as special as Hetty? Grant remembered the locket Hetty wore and the words the engraving stood for. Perhaps they were true.

Continuing onward, Grant returned to planning how he could save Hetty and himself. So caught up in preparation for the upcoming confrontation, Grant missed the storm that suddenly opened up overhead.

Racing toward a line of rocks, he hoped there was an overhang or shallow cave where he and the two horses could get away of the fury crashing around them. Seeing a likely-looking place about four hundred yards farther, Grant raced toward it. Pulling up, Grant and the horses managed to squeeze in just as a streak of lightning cut across the sky, followed immediately by a loud clap of thunder. The sky really opened up, emptying its reservoir of rain.

Twenty minutes later the sun returned, creating diamonds where drops of water remained. These rare gems soon dissolved as the sun warmed, drying out the air.

"If I can get blindsided by a storm, then Boggs could kill me without my being aware," Grant spoke aloud, his voice sounding loud in the quiet, rain-drenched world.

"We'd do well to be on our guard, deal with things as they present themselves," Grant told the horses.

Odysseus nodded his head, and Grant laughed. "I can see why Hetty loves you so much."

Wiping off the saddle, Grant switched over to Nelly, and the trio resumed their journey to Hetty, Boggs or perhaps even their death.

In less than an hour, the described cabin came into sight. It was nestled in a small valley, backing up to a south-facing rise.

Knowing Boggs, Grant began watching for any lookouts who would signal Boggs of his arrival. His, and Hetty's survival—if she truly were a captive—depended on Grant having the upper hand, the element of surprise.

As Grant surveyed the area, he picked out every possible place to watch where someone might be hiding. When he had finished, he had located four possible sites.

Loosely tying off the horses, in case he failed to return, Grant set out to scout each of the four. Using every skill he learned in his twenty-five years, Grant started at the closest.

The first was clear, but the second showed signs of someone having recently been there. Casting about, he saw where the watcher had come and gone at least three times.

*Good chance this one'll be returning*, Grant thought. *Better finish checking the others, then return to take out whoever was here.*

The remaining two sites showed no signs of activity. Grant took a moment to relax his muscles before returning to the one active site.

He had just hidden himself when he heard a sound of someone coming. From the noise the person was making, Grant felt he was probably unaware of his presence.

Grant was getting ready to silence the oncoming lookout, when he felt a hand on his shoulder. Whirling and drawing at the same time, he was tightening his finger on the trigger, when he noticed a badge on the man's chest.

"Davis?" came a whisper.

"Who are you?" Grant asked.

"My name's Will Murphy, Marshal of Kiowa Wells. I've been trying to catch up with you, since Hetty contacted us."

"Us?"

"Yes, myself and US Marshal Taylor Wright. Wright should be arriving shortly, he went to check on someone he's been tracking."

"So what are you doing here?" Grant asked, confusion and hope sparring in his mind. Why would these two lawmen be here, and what was this about Hetty?

Grant saw another man walk up, with a prisoner in custody.

"Is this Davis?" the man asked.

"Sure is, who you got?" Marshal Murphy asked the newcomer.

"Think this is the man who kidnapped our friend Hetty. Horse tracks looked the same, so when he was coming back here, thought I'd just bring him over for some questioning."

At hearing that Hetty had been kidnapped, Grant lunged for the prisoner, "What did you do to her, did you hurt her?" Grant snarled, just before he was pulled away.

"Calm down, Davis, we need to have a plan to not only save Hetty, but to capture Boggs," Wright said.

Realizing he now had help, that Hetty was in fact here, Grant handed the two men the note he'd received directing him here. "If it'll help, here's a copy of the note and map I was given in Leadville."

"Then let's get busy," Marshal Murphy said.

# CHAPTER
## Thirty - Four

S ometimes you just want to spread your wings and
fly away, Hetty thought. Life becomes too harsh,
the situation you perceive you cannot escape. Then
someone shows an unexpected kindness and it's as
precious as water to the thirsty man. Hetty now knew
Boggs was just using her to kill Grant. That he would kill
her also, she was sure. She would do her best to make sure
he failed. She owed it to Grant.

"Won't be long now," came the hated voice in her ear.

"You've been saying that for three days now," Hetty
said as she smiled, her secret smile. "You don't know, do
you?"

As expected, Boggs flew into a rage. The waiting hadn't
been easy for him either. Hetty braced herself for the
onslaught, but it was slow in coming.

"What don't I know?" Boggs growled, a knife pricking
her throat. Hetty knew she had him. She slowly leaned into

the blade. The extra blood caught the man's eye and he drew the blade back. Then a hand connected with her cheek, bringing the beginnings of a horrible bruise.

"Thought you were smart, huh? Well, this time ol' Boggs caught on."

Suddenly Boggs straightened and Hetty rocked the chair toward him. She had heard a noise outside also.

"You witch," Boggs screamed, as he dodged Hetty's falling chair. "You won't succeed, he will die and I'll collect the five thousand dollars." His hand rose, the pistol falling forward. "Then after you watch him die, I'm going to kill you."

She caught the movement of the pistol from the corner of her eye as she lay on the floor. Instead of connecting with her head, it flew backward, followed immediately by the sound of the shot.

"You," Grant yelled at Boggs. Grant fired again, blood spurting out from a hole in Boggs' shoulder.

Grant might have fired again, but Hetty saw Will Murphy and Taylor Wright come through the door.

"Calm down, Davis," Murphy said, his hand on Grant's gun arm.

"You jumped the gun. I've never seen anyone move so fast," Wright added as he moved over to Boggs, turning him and placing the cuffs on his wrist.

"He was going to hurt Hetty, I couldn't let him do that," Grant exclaimed.

Hetty lay on the floor, watching the scene in front of her. She felt she was hallucinating. Grant was here and he was safe, but why were Will and Taylor here? The three day ordeal, along with little water and no food was making it hard to focus. Hetty felt herself fading, she'd nothing left. A whimper escaped her lips.

Grant heard the sound and with a cry, fell to the floor, untying Hetty. "Hetty, Hetty?"

Will and Taylor shared a look, then took Boggs outside to join the other man they'd captured earlier.

"He's got it bad," Taylor said to Will.

"He sure does. Guess we're going to need a new teacher."

The next thing Hetty knew she was in Grant's arms and he was calling her name.

"Grant?"

"I'm here, I'm here," she heard as clear air and a feeling of relief overtook her.

Seeing Grant holding Hetty, Will said, "You two take all the time you need. We'll be heading to Leadville with the prisoners, then the train to Denver."

"Take care," Grant said, looking at Hetty, still in his arms. "Watch out for a man named Swisher, he's the one delivered the note."

"We will, and I suggest you read that letter from your brother, who by the way is on the mend," Will added.

"I would, but I burned it. For now all that matters is Hetty getting better."

"Davis, that letter might be a bit singed, but it's still intact. Hetty sent it to me, and I've placed it in your saddlebags," Will informed Grant. "You take care of Hetty, she's special, and take all the time you need getting to Kiowa Wells."

"Kiowa Wells?"

"It's where Hetty lives, along with my wife, the doctor. And I might add, where your brother is. He's anxious to see you again."

Watching the two officers ride off with their prisoners, Grant thought about what Will had said. He wasn't sure about seeing his brother, but he would do his best to take care of Hetty. She was special, but they did need to talk. But how to approach the subject of his name of outlaw and their marriage?

# CHAPTER
Thirty-Five

G rant sat looking at Hetty as she lay sleeping. He'd made a small fire outside the cabin and made a bed for himself and Hetty. His heart had almost stopped when he'd seen her tied to the chair, Boggs standing beside her, a pistol falling toward her head.

Even now, after it was over, he wished that he could've killed Boggs for what he'd put Hetty through. As much as it might have made him feel better, Grant needed to focus on Hetty. She had been through so much because of him. Would he ever be able to make it up to her?

"Grant, stop feeling guilty," her voice carried over to him.

"But."

"I chose to help you, I saw so much good in you."

Grant stared into the fire. Had he heard correctly, she chose to help him? But if she'd known what might happen, would she still have made the same choice?

Hetty's breath was slow and steady, so Grant wasn't sure if she'd spoken or not. Even so, he began to relax. Even if the words he'd heard were wishful thinking, there seemed to be something he needed to learn.

Despite all he'd been through, Grant knew sleep would not come easy.

*I chose to help you*, continued to repeat itself in Grant's brain. She chose him. Why? He was a man with a reputation, undeserved, yes, but one he carried.

So far, he'd still failed to clear his name. Even if she wished to stay with him, could he ask her to give up the life she built before being forced into his life.

Of course, she did choose to find him and deliver Harry's letter. That same letter he tossed into the fire in what he now realized was a fit of childish anger. It was a bitter lesson, one that was painful.

Somewhere during all his recriminations to himself, Grant fell asleep. He awoke with a start, finding himself lying on the ground with Hetty sitting nearby.

"What?"

"You fell asleep, and since we're still in the wilds, I thought I'd stand guard while you rested."

Grant was quiet. There were things they needed to talk about, but he just didn't know how to start. Instead the two sat in silence. The sun began its rise over the mountains, and the world grew lighter.

Odysseus and Nelly could be heard as they pulled the grass where Grant had picketed them.

Grant wanted to ask Hetty if he'd heard her correctly last night. Yet, as the silence continued, his courage failed. He admitted to himself he was scared of her answer. He looked over to where she sat, watching her face, thinking again how striking, how beautiful she looked.

"You're beautiful, you know," Grant spoke what he thought, surprised when she turned his way.

"Are you making fun of me?"

Grant realized he must've spoken aloud. It hurt that

Hetty didn't believe him. Rising, he moved over to sit beside her.

"Hetty, I would never make fun of you. I don't know where you got the idea, but there is something you need to believe. You truly are beautiful, outside and in."

Hetty looked at Grant, hope, and yes, fear in her eyes. "You truly believe that?"

Taking her hand, Grant pulled her into his arms. "Yes."

Hetty sighed, relaxing into the circle of Grant's arms. She allowed herself to believe his words, to feel treasured and wanted, even if only for these few moments.

The two remained as they were as the day began to grow warm. The sun's beams were breaking over the treetops to shine down, warming the world around them.

"As much as I would like to remain here just holding you, I think we should get started. It's a long trip back to your home."

Hetty jerked back as if slapped. "As you wish."

As they prepared to set out, Hetty avoided Grant to the point that Grant commented, "Are you okay? I know you've been through quite the ordeal."

"I'm fine," Hetty answered, but Grant didn't believe her. Her closed face cut off any further conversation.

Grant searched his mind for an answer to the sudden change in Hetty. As hard as he tried he could not come up with an answer. That he had hurt her, even if unknowingly, gave Grant much to think about as they continued their journey.

# CHAPTER
## Thirty-Six

T hey stopped around noon for a break. Hetty was glad. Despite her comments to the contrary, she was having a hard time staying in the saddle. She was also worried about how to approach the subject of their fake marriage.

"Would you answer a question for me?" Grant's words cut into Hetty's thoughts.

"It depends on the question."

"So that's how it's to be. Fine," Grant snarled, glaring at Hetty.

"Your attitude doesn't encourage cooperation," Hetty retorted, just as a shot echoed through the area.

"You keep that up, Grant. I'm going to kill you," a voice echoed down.

Grant cursed, throwing Hetty to one side behind a large boulder. He turned, firing at the voice. He ducked and was preparing to move toward his attacker. He'd started out, only to be driven back by another shot, followed by another. Grant fired back, preparing to run when Hetty pulled him back.

Grant frowned in frustration. "Why did you pull me back?"

"He's trying to kill you. Don't you care?"

"I was trying to get around him, Frenchy is a very dangerous man."

"Who's Frenchy?"

"The man shooting at us," Grant ground out in frustration.

"Fine, then just go get yourself killed," Hetty retorted as she attempted to stand, only to fall.

"What in tarnation?"

"Nothing," Hetty answered as she gained her feet. She stood, standing with her right side toward Grant, balancing on her left leg.

"Before this goes any further, tell me what's going on." Hetty demanded.

"You know, it's been a long time since I've seen anyone who takes chances the way you do," Grant ground out.

About that time, Frenchy opened up again. "I'm going to kill you for what you did to my wife."

Turning away from Hetty, Grant yelled, "I didn't do anything to you or your wife."

The light in Hetty's eyes should have warned Grant. Placing her hands on her hips, Hetty grabbed Grant, "What is he talking about, and don't change the subject."

"Fine," Grant answered. "Frenchy was in prison the same time I was. When I was in Leadville, after I got out of the hospital..."

"Hospital? Why were you in a hospital?"

Taking a breath and ducking the next barrage, Grant continued, "I was attacked by a mountain lion, I'm fine. But, Frenchy is very jealous of anyone who looks at his wife. He introduced me to her and well, let's just say I got out of there as fast as I could."

Hetty looked at Grant, worry in her eyes. "He'd kill you for..."

"Yes, when he's in this kind of temper. Now, I'll distract him and you get on Odysseus and get out of here."

"What if I..."

Grant wanted to shake some sense into Hetty, but he also admired her fearlessness.

"Please, just do as I say."

Hetty could see Grant was serious. Maybe Frenchy's interference was a blessing to Grant. He could get rid of her and, Hetty didn't want to follow that line of thought. She nodded and when Grant opened up again, she ran for her horse and took off.

Grant stared, she left. He felt empty, but it was better she was gone than run the risk of being shot.

Grant heard the sound of Hetty riding away, then he turned his attention to Frenchy. The two traded shots, until Grant was almost without ammunition.

"You should be about out of bullets." Frenchy shouted. "When you are I'm going to come down there and cut your heart out."

Grant knew, in his present state of mind, he would probably do that. At least Hetty was safe. He was preparing to fire the last of his ammunition, when he heard Hetty's voice.

"You will put down that gun, or I swear I'll shoot it out of your hand."

"Woman, what you..."

"I said, put it down. You should be back with your wife, treating her like she was special instead of chasing after men who you think looked at her. Of all the stupid things to do."

Grant stood transfixed. Hetty had come to his rescue, but what if Frenchy...

# CHAPTER
## Thirty-Seven

H ad Hetty turned in her sleep? Grant watched, making sure she was truly asleep. The day was one of frustration. First she'd been angry at him, then Frenchy had tried to kill them. Then instead of riding to safety, she'd doubled back and sent Frenchy on his way.

They still hadn't been able to talk things out. When Hetty returned, they'd ridden on in silence. When Grant saw how tired Hetty was, he'd called a halt. Hetty, still not speaking, made her bed and was instantly asleep.

Now, that she was back, Grant wasn't sure he could let her go. He was remembering the two of them stealing away from Boggs, and how his actions, his reputation had almost gotten her killed. Even the incident with Frenchy was his fault.

Rising, Grant moved off the short distance, far enough away from Hetty to not disturb her, but close enough to keep watch. He still couldn't believe Harrison's actions, his trying to contact him. Thinking of the letter, Grant went to retrieve it from his saddlebags. Perhaps it was time to see what it said.

Grant turned, feeling a hand on his shoulder. He was frustrated and angry at himself for not hearing anyone approach. He glanced over to where Hetty was sleeping. There was no one there. If someone had…

"Can't sleep?" Came Hetty's gentle question, followed by a comforting arm encircling his waist.

Grant, his defenses down, said to Hetty, "I love you."

"What?" she gasped.

"I said I love you."

"I think you are probably having a relapse. Should we head back to Leadville?"

"Well, if you think I'm ill, just because I..." Grant stopped, looking at Hetty. "Well, since you put it that way, I suppose. But you have to admit you have been acting a bit contrary," Grant grinned.

"I'm not contrary so much as someone who prefers to be treated equally. But, let's…"

"Let's what?" Grant inquired as he moved closer.

"Let's talk about something else."

Silence grew, the wind whistled quietly, the birds chirped as Hetty watched Grant's face. He shut his eyes. She could see determination building. Hetty wondered if he was going to ignore her suggestion when a sigh left him. His eyes opened, he looked at Hetty, then said, "Very well, but we will have this out. Right now, I'm going to read that letter, the one that started all this."

Grant left Hetty standing where she was. He'd told her he loved her, but she didn't believe it. He might not know what was going on, but he would find a way.

For her part, Hetty was feeling guilty at not having told Grant the truth. She did love him, but because the marriage was fake, and he'd done so much, she didn't want to coerce him. How could she keep her heart safe from more hurt when he found out?

Grant returned, letter in hand. Ignoring Hetty, he sat and opened it.

*Grant,*

*I know you can't forgive me for what I did to you. I don't expect it. However, I want you to know, I believed Mother when she said she was only doing this to make you see sense, to stop your wild ways. It was a year later when I learned you'd been sent to prison. I know you wonder how that could be. You know Mother, she gets what she wants.*

*Once I learned about the Will, and then the reward for your death, I finally realized what you always knew, Mother is crazy.*

*I hope this letter gets to you before someone tries to kill you.*

*Forever your loving brother,*

*Harry*

Grant stared at the letter, then the reward poster. Harrison finally knew the truth and tried to make amends. It would take him some time to get over what Harrison had done, but it brought Hetty into his life. Now, he needed to figure out a way to keep her.

# CHAPTER
*Thirty-Eight*

H etty was reciting Homer to Odysseus. Did she do that often? Grant did his best to keep a straight face, but it was fast becoming a losing battle. Hetty was the most irritating, self-contained woman he'd ever met. He admired that she took on the task of finding him, to deliver his brother's letter. That she'd almost lost her life in doing so, that was something he would never forget. Yet, somewhere, at some time, she'd built a wall around herself. A wall behind which she kept herself safe. Well, he just had to find a way to knock down that wall. She didn't realize she was perfection. Yes, she was perfect for him.

"Why are you smirking?" Hetty asked, eyes flashing gold daggers.

"Who me? I'm just listening to you recite the classics to your horse."

Hetty glared at Grant, then she slowly advanced toward

him. If he didn't watch out, he could find himself in the situation that might deteriorate very quickly.

Smiling, Grant said, "By the way, I always enjoyed that one. I always regretted losing my copy."

His words stopped Hetty in her tracks. That Grant had an education she knew, but he liked her favorite story.

"When did you have time to read Homer?" Hetty started, only to stop as she realized what a personal and judgmental question it was.

"I made time," Grant grinned, then continued. "One summer, I had some free time. There wasn't much available to read, just a copy of Homer's Odyssey. I soon found myself relating to the character in the story."

Hetty felt herself liking this contrary man even more.

"It's the story of all people, their journey, it's just a different time is all," Grant finished.

"That's the way I see it also," Hetty responded. "I do confess that the wife had it tough staying home, but I always related to the hero."

Grant grinned, he understood. He felt that way, too. Who would've thought out here in the middle of nowhere he could find something Hetty and he shared from their earlier lives?

"You're deep in thought," Hetty's words broke through Grant's ruminations. "Anything I need to know?"

"Hetty, you need to trust me. I won't lie to you."

Hetty paused, he was right, she needed to trust him. If they were to succeed in working this out, trust was going to have to start somewhere.

"Grant, I need to tell you," Hetty stopped, her eyes taking in the sun as it made its way west. The old saying popped into her head. Red sky at night, sailors delight, Red sky in morning, sailor's warning. The sky was red in the west. Was that a sign?

"What?"

Hetty pulled her eyes away from the sky, turning her gaze to Grant. "When Boggs had me prisoner, he laughed at our being married. He said he hadn't believed our story, and the marriage ceremony that he put us through was a fake."

"You sure?" Grant asked. "He put you through so much. Are you sure you heard correctly?"

"I know he was telling the truth. He had no need to lie. It was one more thing to make me feel badly. I knew he was going to kill me after he had killed you."

Grant hurt for Hetty, for what she was saying. His mind grasping at the horror of what she'd endured, as she continued.

"He called me loose, ugly and then he acted like he was going to kiss me, only to almost suffocate me."

"Hetty..." Grant started.

"I knew the truth then, no one would ever want me. I only wanted to live long enough to try and save you, but I even failed at that."

"Hetty, look at me," Grant demanded.

Hetty turned toward Grant, a numb pain coursing through her.

"I asked you to trust me, and do you?"

For the longest time Grant was afraid Hetty wouldn't answer. Then when he was ready to give up, she whispered, "Yes."

Grant pulled Hetty to him. He got down on one knee. "Hetty Osgood, you have saved me. You've shown me not only what love is, but that I'm capable of loving someone with all my heart and soul. You would make me the happiest and luckiest man in the world if you would stay with me," Grant looked into Hetty's eyes. "Marry me?"

Grant paused, waiting for Hetty to speak. His heart almost burst when she knelt down next to him. "I love you, and, yes, I will marry you."

"Even someone with the label of 'outlaw'?"

"Even then."

Grant pulled Hetty close, his arms holding her to his heart. Leaning in, he kissed her with all the love he'd been holding behind his own wall of protection. They would have some good and bad times in the coming years, but they would have each other.

"Well then, wife, because to me you are and ever will be my wife," Grant said. "Let's head home and have a real wedding."

# EPILOGUE

J uly 4, 1880, was a day of celebration in Kiowa Wells. Firecrackers popped, horses raced as the community celebrated the beginning of the country. The town was dressed in its finest regalia as people from the surrounding communities arrived for the big day.

Doc Brown traveled from Canyon City, bringing Maude and her son Clover. Many noted the good doctor discussing illness and treatments with their own Doc Josie.

The big parade made its way down Main Street to the church at the end of town. There, everyone gathered for the wedding of their beloved teacher.

At the front of the church stood Grant, beside him his brother Harrison. Harrison, although looking pale and feeling weak, had insisted on standing up with his brother.

Just before the bride arrived, Harrison addressed the crowd. "There are some who say my brother is an outlaw. There is nothing further from the truth. He was, is and always has been a man of character. I wish he and his soon-to-be-bride all the best, and request each and every one of you still any talk of Grant being anything other than honest and the best of men."

Grant leaned over, giving his brother a hug, then turned as Hetty came down the aisle on the arm of Marshal Will Murphy. Any who saw the look on Grant's face knew he adored and cherished his bride-to-be.

After the ceremony, the bride and groom led the way to the overflowing picnic tables. There, the couple shared in the laughter. When it was time to leave for Grant,'s home, the couple mounted up on Odysseus and Nelly, waving their goodbyes. Harrison would join them when he was able to travel.

As the two rode away, many swore they heard laughter, and the two quoting Homer to each other.

Thank you for reading

## THE OUTLAW'S LETTER

Each book in the
**Lockets & Lace**
series is a Clean, Sweet Historical Romance. You may find
all the books in this series as they are published by
searching for

**"Lockets and Lace"** on **Amazon.com**

If you enjoyed this book, please help other readers find it
by leaving a review on
**Amazon Review**
and
**Goodreads**.

Just a few words will do. Reviews make *all* the difference!

To learn more about the Sweet Americana Sweethearts
blog, our authors, and our individual books, please visit

**SweetAmericanaSweethearts.blogspot.com**

Lockets & Lace Books
by
Sweet Americana Sweethearts Blog Authors:

# OTHER ANGELA RAINES BOOKS

### Josie's Dream

*Dr. Josephine Forrester always dreamed of being a doctor. That dream did not include a husband until William Murphy showed up.*

### Chasing a Chance

*Edwin Markham thought he'd lost his first and one true love, Mary Gilpin when she married another when he went off to war. But the fates had other ideas in store for these two.*

### The Agate Gulch Stories:
Home for His Heart,
Never Had A Chance,
Gift of Forgiveness

*Join the people of Agate Gulch Colorado as they live, love and find their way in the mountains and plains of Colorado.*

www.ingramcontent.com/pod-product-compliance
Lightning Source LLC
Chambersburg PA
CBHW021153130626
46554CB00005B/1788